The Time Traveller and the TIGER

Also by Tania Unsworth

The Girl Who Thought Her Mother Was a Mermaid

Tania Unsworth

The Time Traveller and the TIGER

ZEPHYR

An imprint of Head of Zeus

For David Emile Thaler,
always and forever.

PART 1:

The Tiger in the Spare Room

One

1946. CENTRAL INDIA.

It was so still, John was sure it was dead.

He didn't know how long he'd been standing there, rigid with shock and disbelief. The birds had risen shrieking from the trees and answering cries of alarm had filled the forest. Now a hush had fallen over the clearing. John stepped forward, still holding the gun in both hands, his eyes locked on the body in the grass. It lay with its back to him, its colour even more improbable in the hard, open glare of the midday sun. He took a few more steps and stopped, his heart thudding. Insects pulsed steadily in the undergrowth and an invisible woodpecker tapped, paused, and tapped again.

John leaned closer, craning his neck.

The tiger snarled and twisted with shocking ferocity, striking too fast for John to see. He felt his feet leave the ground; a confusion of sky, muscled fur and burning breath. Then pain tore through his body, and the world went out.

It was dark when he opened his eyes. He was half on his back, half on his side. There were stars in the sky, and in the corner of his vision, the black shapes of trees. His gun lay nearby, moonlight glinting on the barrel, although he couldn't reach it. Something hot and vastly heavy was preventing him from moving his legs. He raised his head.

His heart staggered and seemed to stop.

The tiger was lying on top of him, pinning him from the waist down. John could smell the sharp, musky, overpowering scent of its skin, could see the slope of its back, ten shades darker than the night sky. As he stared, the slope rose a fraction and he felt a shudder run through the tiger's body.

It was still alive!

Every atom in John's body froze. Then his heart bounded into frenzy, and the stars above him trembled, as if the sky itself was being shaken. Any second now, the tiger would turn and kill him. John wished he was already dead, just to have it over and done with, just to stop the awful pounding in his chest. With a great effort, he managed to raise his right hand. He clutched the front of his shirt and waited.

Nothing moved. Only the cold night breeze in the grass, and the slope of the tiger's back as it breathed.

No tiger lay out in the open, especially one that was wounded. John didn't need Mandeep to tell him that. It would drag itself to cover if it could. He felt another breath fill the tiger's body and pass slowly away.

The animal was too hurt to seek refuge. It couldn't move, any more than he could. They were in the same boat, the tiger and him. For a second, John had an image of a fishing vessel with narrow hull and snug canopy, the tiger steering with a long oar at the stern, while John kept watch at the bow. The image was so clear and so bizarre, he felt a spark of hope. Perhaps he was dreaming. Fast asleep under a mosquito net in his bedroom at home. Safe.

Then the pain came back. It came suddenly, as

if – like the tiger – it had been waiting to strike, spreading from his right leg in a knife-sharpened wave. He heard himself groan, and as if in answer, the distant *whoop-whoop* of langur monkeys. The sky blurred.

Time passed. He couldn't tell if it was a minute or an hour. He found the pain was slightly less if he twisted his shoulder to one side. He grabbed a clump of grass to hold himself in place and clenched his teeth.

His leg must be broken, he thought. It was a miracle he wasn't dead. The tiger could have killed him easily. Mandeep said…

His head swam, his hold on the grass slippery with sweat.

Mandeep said that a tiger's forepaw was powerful enough to knock a full-grown bull off its feet, and deft enough to catch a passing fly. Once, during a hunt, a tiger had sprung from the bushes and leaped over the head of one of the beaters. It had barely brushed the man as it passed. Yet when the others went to help the beater to his feet, they found him dead. The tiger had snapped his neck as if it were a twig.

If a tiger wants to kill you, Mandeep had once told John, there is no power on earth that can stop it.

It didn't want to kill me, John thought. *It was only defending itself.*

His mind wandered. Back at home they would have missed him by nightfall, although it would have been pointless to send a search party. They would be waiting for first light before setting out to look for him. By then it might be too late. John wondered how his parents would feel if he died. Sad, of course. But mostly disappointed at how badly he had let them down.

The pain had grown distant. In its place was a creeping chill, as if his bones were turning to ice.

He stared at the tiger's dark bulk. Its breath seemed slower than before, and he found himself counting each rise and fall.

One... two...

Perhaps if he tried, he could count them in to morning, he and the tiger, together in the same boat.

Eight... nine...

The boat had a blue canopy; water droplets flew, sparkling as the long oar dipped. All he had to do was concentrate, and he could count them in to shore, across the teeming, earth-brown river.

John had loosened his grip on the clump of grass some time ago. Now, barely knowing what he was doing, he lifted his hand and placed it on the tiger's back, palm flat against the warm, silky hide.

Thirty-seven... thirty...

The sky grew pearly and the low mist of dawn gathered above the tall grasses, turning their tips to silver. The sound of birds filled the air with a hundred different trills and babbles and whistling calls. But John was hardly aware of any of it. Somewhere, between one number and the next, he had hesitated. He had lost count. And now there was no point starting again.

The tiger lay still beneath his hand.

Far above, a vulture circled on broad, unhurried wings. John followed it with his eyes, feeling his mind drift from his body. He was with the vulture, looking down on himself. He saw his own face turned to the sky, saw the motionless body of the tiger. It looked far smaller than he remembered, already turning pale. The living flame of its skin fading to the colour of grass at the end of summer.

A terrible grief filled John's heart. A sense of wrongness that could never be put right. Tears rose in his eyes and ran unchecked down the side of his face. He heard a cry, the thump of running feet. The men in the search party were here. Mandeep was leaning over him, touching his hand.

John tried to speak but no words came.

'Be still,' Mandeep said.

He was carried home, one of the servants running ahead to fetch the doctor from town. His broken leg would never fully heal. He would always walk with a limp, although in time he would get used to it. In time, he would get used to many things. A new home, a new country, a different way of thinking about the world.

But all his life – even when he was an old man – he would carry the sense of wrongness he'd felt that morning when the tiger died. As if something had happened which wasn't meant to happen. As if a mistake had been made in the universe. And because of it, he would live his life the same way he walked.

Always just a little out of step.

Two

THE PRESENT. ENGLAND.

There was a tiger in Great-Uncle John Lassiter's other spare room.

Elsie nearly screamed when she opened the door. Then she saw it wasn't a tiger. It was just something that had once been one. Now it lay with its empty legs spread out, as flat and as dry as a great, striped flower pressed between the pages of a book. Only its head had been left intact, its jaws frozen in a roar.

There wasn't anything else in the room, apart from a glass cabinet full of what looked like a hundred identical cups and saucers. Elsie walked all the way around the tiger, gazing at it. Then, holding her breath, she bent and touched its head with the tip of her finger.

The tiger's eyes were made of glass, fixed in a dull stare.

Elsie went back into the corridor. She could hear her great-uncle in the kitchen, clattering pans as he made breakfast. Any minute now, he would call her, and she would have to go and make conversation. With a perfect stranger. Who had a dead tiger in his spare room.

If only her mother hadn't forgotten Elsie was meant to be on holiday.

'I don't know how I got the dates wrong,' her mother had said for the twentieth time, on the long drive to Great-Uncle John's house the day before. 'I thought your holidays started *next* week.'

Elsie didn't say anything. She was used to people forgetting about her. It happened quite a lot. Just last week, after the school trip to the wildlife centre, the coach taking them back had left without her. It was seventeen whole minutes before anyone noticed. She had spent the time sitting on a bench by the centre's entrance, trying to think cheerful thoughts. *It's funny, really,* she had decided. *It's an adventure!*

Elsie supposed she must be easy to overlook because she was so small. And also because, apart from that, there wasn't a single thing about her that stood out. She was neither at the top of the class, nor the bottom. She wasn't great at sports, and she wasn't hopeless. She wasn't popular or unpopular, bold or timid, pretty or plain.

If she was in a film, Elsie thought, she would be an extra; one of those people who wandered around in the background, while the main character was having a fascinating conversation, or fighting villains, or just walking down the street in the way that main characters did. As if their outline was twice as clear as everyone else's.

'I know you're going to like your great-uncle,' Elsie's mother said.

'But I've never even met him,' Elsie said.

'Well, of course you have! Your father and I were staying with him when you were born. He chose your name. His mother – your great-great-aunt – was called Elsie. We visited him a lot when you were tiny, before we went to live in Boston.'

Elsie didn't remember. She had spent most of her

life in America. Her parents had decided to move back to England only last year.

'I don't see why I can't go with you to your conference.'

'We've been through this already,' her mother said. 'You'd have nothing to do and I can't cancel any of my meetings. Plus, your dad won't be back from his business trip until the middle of next week... it's awful timing...'

Elsie sighed and bent her head to her notebook again, her pen moving rapidly over the page as her mother talked.

The Incredible Adventures of Kelsie Corvette

When Kelsie Corvette was born her parents were so happy they wished every day of the year could be her birthday and they always planned fantastic summer holidays for her even though they weren't very ~~afloo~~ aflew

'How do you spell "affluent"?' Elsie said.

'Are you listening to me?' her mother said. 'I was

telling you about Great-Uncle John. He's such a kind man, I've always wondered why he never married. My mother told me there was a girl he liked, years and years ago, but for some reason it didn't work out, and he never fell in love with anyone else. But that's John for you. He can be very stubborn once he gets an idea in his head…'

Elsie stared out of the car window, biting the top of her pen.

We have a lovely surprise for you Kelsie her mum said one day. How would you like to spend the summer on a ranch in Texas? Kelsie had never ridden a horse before but as she rose in the saddle she instinktivly knew what to do. I've never seen anything like it said the owner of the ranch she's a natural. One of my men was bitten by a rattelsnake can you take his place in the rodeo next week?

Not a problem! said Kelsie Corvette.

'I don't know how I got the dates wrong,' Elsie's mother said for the twenty-first time. 'I'm really, really sorry.'

'It's okay,' Elsie told her. 'It's only for a week. Maybe it'll be interesting.'

Her mother gave her a grateful look. 'You're so good at making the best of things, Elsie,' she said.

Three

*E*lsie went to her room and got dressed. Her jeans were too long for her. She'd had to fold the bottoms to make them fit. The extra rolls of denim gave her legs a cut-off look, as if she was wading up to her ankles.

On the plus side, it was surprising how many things you could store in the turn-ups. They were almost as good as pockets, Elsie thought.

Great-Uncle John had made eggs and bacon and baked beans and fried tomatoes and toast for breakfast.

'I got extra bacon,' he said. 'I thought, everyone likes bacon, don't they?'

Elsie nodded, staring at the table. There was so much food that she could hardly see her plate.

'You can't go wrong with bacon,' Great-Uncle John said.

'I guess not,' Elsie said, trying to load her fork without sending an egg sliding on to the tablecloth. The table had been set with napkins, a vase of flowers, a butter dish in the shape of a cow, and a pair of salt and pepper shakers that looked as if they were made of solid silver. Great-Uncle John had gone to a lot of trouble just for breakfast, she thought.

She gave him a quick glance as he went to fetch milk from the fridge. He was thin, with quite a lot of hair left, and although he walked with a limp, he didn't hobble or take ages to get from one side of the kitchen to the other. For someone so old, he looked fairly normal, she decided.

He sat down at the table and cleared his throat. Elsie wondered if he was going to say something about bacon again. She had the feeling he was finding it as difficult to make conversation as she was.

'This is delicious,' she said, to be helpful. 'Thank you, Great-Uncle John.'

'That's a bit of a mouthful, isn't it?' he said. 'Maybe you could just call me...' He paused.

'Perhaps "Uncle John" would be easier,' he suggested, after deep thought.

'Okay.'

Another silence fell. 'I hope you won't find it too dull, staying here,' he said. 'I don't suppose it's quite how you imagined spending the summer holidays. The village is rather small, but of course there's always the woods, and the river, and so on…' His voice trailed off.

'It sounds really nice,' Elsie said. 'I like exploring.'

'After breakfast, I'll give you a tour of the house. So you'll know where everything is.'

'I've already looked upstairs,' Elsie admitted. She hesitated. 'Did that… tiger come from India?'

Elsie's mother had told her that John had lived in India when he was a boy, when the country was still ruled by the British, so she thought it was probably a good guess.

He nodded. 'It did, yes.'

Elsie thought of the tiger's roaring mouth. It was meant to be frightening, yet it just looked strange and sad.

'Why do you keep it in that room?'

The lines in Uncle John's forehead seemed to deepen. He was silent for so long that Elsie thought he wasn't going to answer.

'I have to keep it because I was the one who killed it,' he said at last. 'I shot it when I was twelve years old.'

Elsie stared at him.

'It was the worst thing I ever did,' Uncle John said.

Four

Kelsie soon got the hang of the rodeo. Everyone's eyes were fixed on her tall graceful figure as she galloped into the ring and swung her lassoo at a—

'Do you think it hurts cattle when they get lassoed at rodeos?' Elsie asked Uncle John, as they sat in the living room that afternoon.

'Probably not. I suppose they get rather used to it.'

Elsie liked the way he didn't appear surprised by the question.

'But they also do it to calves which doesn't seem fair,' Elsie said. 'Calves must be easy to catch.'

'Calves are pretty nimble,' he said. 'I expect they run around a lot.'

Uncle John seemed to take everything she said very seriously. Elsie liked that too.

After breakfast, he had shown her around the house, and then they had taken a walk through the village. Elsie couldn't help her heart sinking at the sight of it. It was so quiet. Nobody stirred to open a door, or raise a window, or stroll down the main street. The only thing that moved was the stream, running under a stone bridge in the village centre.

They came to a broad, grassy hill sloping above the village. At the base of the hill there was a stretch of railway track, overgrown with weeds and stringy-looking grass.

'Doesn't the train come through here any more?' Elsie asked.

Uncle John shook his head. 'They closed the line a while back. But it was always a dangerous place. A long time ago, a little boy was killed by a train not far from here.'

'That's terrible.'

'He was only two years old,' Uncle John said. 'He'd wandered off from his babysitter and somehow found his way on to the tracks.'

Uncle John pointed to a line of trees at the top of the hill. 'I was walking in those woods when it happened…'

'It must have been awful,' Elsie said.

Uncle John gave her a worried look. 'Well, as I said, it was a long time ago. Perhaps we should be getting back. How does a cup of tea sound? I have three different kinds of biscuits.'

'That's nice,' Elsie said, although she felt certain it was only about five minutes since they'd had breakfast.

'You can't go wrong with biscuits,' Uncle John said.

Five

For someone who was so old, Uncle John didn't own many things. Most people's homes were full of stuff. Knick-knacks, fancy cushions, souvenirs from places they'd visited. Uncle John's house was so empty, it made what he did have stand out. A painting of old wooden boats on a river, a framed certificate from when he became a doctor, a pair of curved knives with polished black handles hanging on the wall above the fireplace.

'They're ceremonial Gurkha knives,' he told her. 'My father was presented with them in India. He was in the army, you know.'

'Why?'

'Well, a lot of people went into the army in those days.'

'No, why was he presented with them?'

'Oh.' Uncle John paused. 'I have absolutely no idea,' he said.

After she drank her tea, Elsie went to explore the back garden. It was large, with a lot of rose bushes and a lawn that led downhill to the stream. Elsie stood on the bank, staring at the brown, fast-flowing water. She had hoped she might go swimming, but she saw it was too shallow for that.

She could paddle at least, although she thought she ought to save that for the next day. There was so little to do at Uncle John's house that any activity – even paddling – would have to be strictly rationed. And looking forward to something always made it a bit more fun.

She sighed. Kelsie Corvette never had to invent things to look forward to. Or paddle, for that matter. In chapter fifteen of *The Incredible Adventures* – for a dare – Kelsie had swum all the way across a lake, and then – for another dare – swum all the way back again.

Elsie trudged up the lawn. As she approached, Uncle John came out with a watering can. Elsie followed him around the side of the house.

He had gone into a greenhouse. Elsie gasped when she peeped around the door. The greenhouse was as crowded as the main house was empty. She could hardly see Uncle John among all the ferns and leaves. The air was warm and wet and filled with the overpowering scent of flowers.

'Did you… grow all this stuff?' Elsie asked.

'I don't really have to do much, apart from watering,' he said, although there was a pleased look on his face.

'It smells lovely.'

'That's probably the jasmine,' he said, showing her a cluster of tiny white flowers. 'This variety is called "Belle of India". Over there is oleander, which also has a strong fragrance. My mother used to grow it in our garden. Also, marigolds, although those spread *everywhere*…'

'Are all these plants from India?'

'I suppose so,' he said. 'Almost everything grows there, you know.'

He put down his watering can and limped to a row of pots on the far side of the greenhouse. 'These are orchids,' he said. 'I'm not having a great deal of luck with them.'

They weren't much more than yellowish stalks, Elsie thought, although she was too polite to point it out.

'One of them did produce a bud a few years back,' he said. 'So there's reason to hope.'

Her mother was right. Uncle John could be stubborn once he got an idea in his head.

'Is there anything in here?' Elsie pointed to a larger pot, filled almost to the brim with soil.

Uncle John smiled. 'Yes. A seed. I planted it more than seventy years ago.'

Even for Uncle John, this was taking stubbornness a bit far, Elsie thought.

'Shouldn't it have... done something by now?'

He shook his head, still smiling. 'It's from a rather special plant. They say it only grows once in a person's lifetime. The seed lies in the ground for decades, dry and seemingly dead. Then it sprouts and flowers all in a single night. I've never seen it myself, so I don't know if it's true. It's extremely rare, possibly the rarest plant in the world.'

Elsie stared into the pot. 'Where did you get the seed?'

'I was given it by a friend, on my very last day in India. His name was Mandeep. He pressed it into my hand as we said goodbye. It was said to have strange powers, he told me. Its name means "the flower that catches time".'

'Why did he give it to you?'

'I think he wanted to make sure I would always remember that moment,' Uncle John said. 'Not that I could ever forget. He was more of a brother than a friend, you see. You could say we grew up together.'

'What happened to him?'

'I don't know.' Uncle John's eyes were sad. 'I never saw him again.'

Six

*E*lsie's mother called that evening to see how she was getting on.

'Good,' Elsie said. 'We're watching TV.'

She had seen the film before, although it still didn't make much sense the second time around. A lot of men wearing kilts sat in a castle arguing with each other. Then there was a battle in which everyone died except the main characters.

Elsie wondered if the others knew in advance that they were only going to last three minutes before getting hit by an arrow. She thought they probably did. There was something almost cheerful about the way they yelled as they ran to their doom. As if they knew they had to make the best of it.

They were like the kids in her school who had

to stand at the back of the choir with smiles on their faces, even though all they were allowed to do was hum.

Elsie knew exactly what that felt like.

On the first day of rehearsals for the school concert, she had started out in the front row.

'*There's a dark and a troubled side of life*,' she had sung. '*There's a bright and a sunny side too.*'

The song began slowly, then built to a rousing chorus. Elsie raised her voice enthusiastically.

'*Keep on the sunny side! Always on the sunny side! Keep on the sunny side of —*'

A pained expression crossed the face of Mr Nunes, the music teacher. He gestured for silence.

'It's a difficult tune,' he said, looking at Elsie. 'Perhaps it would be better if you hummed instead.'

And she had to go and stand at the back with all the other hummers.

That evening, in chapter twenty-six of *The Incredible Adventures* a similar thing happened to Kelsie Corvette. Except that out of everyone in the choir, she was the only person who *didn't* have to hum.

You are so good you make the rest sound dingy, Mr N said. A look of awe crossed his normally critickal features. Your voice could tame the heart of even the most savidge beast it makes me want to cry from happyness...

In the film, the men in kilts were still fighting. Elsie glanced at Uncle John in the armchair opposite. He looked as if he had fallen asleep.

'Uncle John?' she whispered.

He gave an odd, startled sound that made Elsie feel embarrassed and sorry for him at the same time.

'Just resting my eyes,' he said. He looked at the slow-ticking clock on the mantelpiece. 'Perhaps it's time to turn in.'

'Okay,' Elsie said, although it was only eight-thirty.

There was a group of photographs arranged next to the clock. She saw a familiar face. 'That's Mum!' she said. 'And me when I was a baby.'

'It was taken just after you were born,' Uncle John said.

Her mother looked as if she had fallen downstairs, Elsie thought.

'Those are my parents,' Uncle John said, pointing to a faded, yellowish picture. They were standing stiffly side by side, the woman dressed in white, the man in a belted jacket, his eyes hidden under the brim of a rigid, bowl-shaped hat.

'It's a solar topee,' Uncle John told her. 'We had to wear them in India, whenever we went out.'

'Who's that?' Elsie pointed to the only other photograph on the mantelpiece, a black-and-white portrait of a young woman sitting on top of a gate. She was wearing a flowery dress, very narrow at the waist, and old-fashioned shoes. Her hair had been set in neat waves, although a strand had come loose in the wind, and her hand was raised as if to brush it off her face.

It was a lovely picture, partly because the woman was so pretty, but mostly, Elsie thought, because she seemed so *fun*. She looked as if she was about to burst into laughter or jump up and do a handstand on top of the gate.

'That's Colleen,' Uncle John said.

There was such meaning in his voice when he said the name that Elsie was suddenly sure this was the girl her mother had told her about in the car. The one Uncle John had wanted to marry.

'I haven't seen her in nearly sixty-four years.'

'Why not?'

He glanced away, his mouth tight. 'The little boy who was killed by the train was her nephew,' he said. 'She was the one babysitting him that day. Her family left the village shortly after, and never came back. Too many memories, I suppose.'

'You could try looking her up on Facebook,' Elsie ventured, in an effort to lift his spirits. Old people liked looking up other old people on Facebook.

He looked at her. 'Yes, there's always that,' he said with a smile.

She followed him as he went up the stairs. The door to the spare room was still closed. Elsie thought of the tiger's glass eyes, pinned in sightless gaze on the other side.

'Uncle John, can I ask you something?'

'Of course.'

'If killing that tiger was the worst thing you ever did, why did you do it?'

He nodded, as if he'd been expecting the question. 'I didn't think the tiger was going to be there,' he said. 'I ought to have done. I'd been tracking it all morning. But somehow, I didn't believe I'd actually *find* it. And suddenly there it was. It wasn't looking at me or going anywhere. It was just standing. As if it was in a dream... or I was.'

He paused. 'It wasn't until I heard the shot, and saw it go down, that I fully understood it was real. Does that make sense to you?'

'I don't know,' Elsie said.

'That's a good answer,' he said. 'I'm not sure it makes sense to me either.'

Seven

The problem with going to bed early, Elsie thought, was that you woke up early too. It was still dark, although when she looked through the curtains, she could see dawn wasn't far away. The sky was growing grey above the distant woods.

She put on her clothes and crept downstairs, pausing at every creak in the floorboards. In the kitchen, she hesitated, wondering if she could make a cup of tea. The kettle was already on the stove. It was one of those old-fashioned stoves that you had to light by hand. Elsie fished in the drawer for a box of matches before realising that she hadn't filled the kettle. She picked it up and took it to the sink.

The kitchen was at the side of the house. Through the window above the sink she could see the path and the front of the greenhouse, the panes bright with early morning light.

The door of the greenhouse was slightly open.

It wasn't important, Elsie thought. Then she remembered Uncle John's struggle with the orchids. The delicate plants might be damaged if they got chilled. She slipped her bare feet into her trainers, grabbed her jumper hanging over the back of a chair and went outside. It was colder than she expected. She hurried down the path.

A broom that had been leaning against the side of the greenhouse had slipped. The handle was wedged half-in, half-out of the door. Elsie bent to pick it up, opening the door wider, and casting an anxious glance inside.

The damp air had a milky sheen, the plants shrouded in a light mist. She straightened up, staring. Through the fronds of palm and trailing fern, she had a clear view to the other side of the greenhouse, to the orchids and Uncle John's empty pot.

It was no longer empty.

Elsie approached it, wondering if she was mistaken. But it was the same pot, the same glazed sides and weathered rim. Two broad, waxy green leaves had appeared from the dry earth. Between them, a solitary flower, shaped like a lily.

It was blue, the way hills are blue. When they are so far away, they have almost turned to sky.

She had to tell Uncle John. She had to run and get him out of bed. But Elsie couldn't move.

The flower had a single petal, curled in a spiral. The more Elsie stared at it, the more it reminded her of those optical illusions which always – no matter how hard you try – lead your eye right back to where you started. What made it more confusing was that instead of growing darker towards the centre, like most flowers, this one grew lighter.

Perhaps that was why it seemed so much bigger on the inside than the outside, she thought.

The flower had a strange scent. Elsie didn't know what it reminded her of, or even how she would describe it. It was both extraordinarily sweet, and

extraordinarily bitter. Yet instead of cancelling each other out, each element seemed only to increase the strength of the other...

She had to get Uncle John. She had to fetch him *now*.

Elsie bent her face close, inhaling the scent again. *The flower that catches time.*

Could *that* be what she was smelling? Elsie wondered. Could it be time itself?

PART 2:

The Flower that Catches Time

Eight

1946. CENTRAL INDIA.

*E*verything was the same. Except there was more of it.

It was warmer, and ten times brighter, and the plants on all sides seemed to have grown clean out of their pots. The ficus shrub on Elsie's right was as tall as a tree. She took a step backwards.

It wasn't as tall as a tree. It *was* a tree. There was another behind it. Uncle John's orchids had escaped and were running up the branches. A bird whistled.

Elsie felt a stab of alarm, thinking of it trapped against the greenhouse glass. Then she saw there was no glass. She whirled around. There was no

broom handle holding the door open. No door either. Only a track curving away, dappled with the shadows of trees.

The plants weren't from India. They appeared to be actually *in* India.

It was very quiet. The steady rasp of insects and the trill of a far-off bird only intensifying the silence.

Elsie's eyes widened, her gaze darting from tree to tree, her mind paralysed by disbelief. Then she took a juddering breath and tried to gather her senses. She knew she wasn't dreaming. But perhaps it would be best to tell herself she was. It was all a dream. Waking up, filling the kettle, seeing the open door of the greenhouse...

Something stung her arm. She slapped it automatically.

'Ouch!' she said out loud.

It was a very life-like dream, she thought, examining the spot of blood above her elbow.

She heard a steady, drumming sound. Someone was running down the track towards her, although they were moving so fast that, for a second, she couldn't make out who it was. Then she saw a boy. He stopped and stood still, staring.

He was wearing a long-sleeved shirt, khaki shorts and woollen, knee-high socks. A bag was strapped across his chest, and a rifle hung from his shoulder. But what Elsie mostly noticed was how thin he was. He could have run a finger around his shirt collar without once touching his neck. The widest parts of his whole body were his knobbly knees.

'What on earth are you doing?' he said.

Elsie didn't know how to answer this.

The boy stepped forward. He was carrying a hat. It looked like the one in the photograph on Uncle John's mantelpiece.

'Where did you come from?' he demanded.

Elsie hesitated. 'England?' she ventured.

'Oh, you must've come out for the hols,' he said. 'Where do your folks live?'

'I'm… not sure.'

'Lost, are you? Is it your first time out here?'

'Yes,' Elsie said.

'I expect you couldn't come out till now, because of the war.'

'Yes,' Elsie said again, although she had no idea what he was talking about. She had decided her best strategy was to agree with everything. That way, she would make sense at least half the time.

'I don't know how—' The boy broke off, staring at Elsie's feet. 'I say, does everyone in England wear shoes like that?'

Elsie glanced at her trainers.

'Yes.'

'Well, I can't stand around all day talking to a girl.' He squared his bony shoulders. 'You'll have to find your own way back.'

'I don't know how.'

He pointed to the track behind him. 'Keep going six or seven miles, you'll get to town.'

'Six or seven *miles*?'

He tugged the strap of his rifle back into place. Elsie noticed initials carved into the wooden stock. *J.L.*

'Is that your gun?' she asked. An astounding – and disturbing – suspicion had begun to form in her mind.

The boy nodded. Elsie searched his narrow,

sweaty face, trying to find anything she recognised. There was nothing, except perhaps a faint resemblance around the eyes…

'So, those initials… they're yours?'

'Whose else would they be?' He peered at her. 'Are you all right?' he said. 'You look frightfully pale.'

Elsie *felt* frightfully pale. She couldn't go on pretending to herself that this was a dream. Somehow, the flower that catches time had caught her too.

'How old are you?' she asked, her voice faint.

'Twelve. I don't know what you're getting at with all these questions.'

Twelve? Elsie struggled with the maths, the numbers slipping in and out of place. 1975? 1846? The last one sounded right. No, she was off by a hundred years. 1946.

'What… are you going to do with the gun?' she faltered.

'I'm going to bag a tiger.'

'Oh no!' Elsie cried, before she could stop herself. 'No! You *can't*.'

Nine

*I*t was one thing to go back in time seventy-four years. But finding yourself in conversation with your own great-uncle was quite another. Especially when he was staring at you with a look of scorn on his twelve-year-old face.

'You must have sunstroke,' John said. 'That's what you get for wandering around without a topee. How old are you anyway? Six?'

'I'm eleven.'

'Bit short, aren't you?'

This was rich, Elsie thought, coming from someone who had to wrap their belt twice around their waist to keep their shorts up. But she decided it would be better to say nothing.

'What's your name?' he asked.

Elsie hesitated. It had occurred to her that if Great-Uncle John was only twelve years old, he wasn't her great-uncle yet. Or even her uncle. Her parents hadn't been born, which meant that, strictly speaking, Elsie herself didn't exist.

She could be anyone at all.

'My name's…'

'What?'

'Kelsie,' she muttered.

'What did you say?'

'Kelsie,' Elsie said in a louder voice. 'Kelsie Corvette.'

'Kelsie Corvette?' he repeated. 'That sounds made-up.'

'Well, it isn't,' Elsie said.

He tugged at his rifle strap again. 'I've wasted enough time. You ought to be cutting off home.'

'But I don't know how.'

'I told you, follow the track.'

'Wait!' But he was already jogging away, his bag bouncing against his back. Elsie watched as he turned the bend and disappeared from view.

She looked up. Even filtered by trees, the sun felt

hot. After taking off her jumper and tying it around her waist, she found a bush with large, spreading leaves, tugged one free, and attached it to her head with a piece of grass. It wasn't much of a hat; it kept slipping over her eyes, and the grass was already starting to feel itchy. But it was better than nothing.

She drew a deep breath. Then she plodded off in the direction that John had taken, the roll-ups of her jeans chafing her hot legs.

It seemed that, sometimes, even Kelsie Corvette had to make the best of things.

John must have picked up speed. When Elsie reached the bend, he was nowhere in sight. It was darker ahead. On one side of the track, the ground sloped steeply upwards into dense thicket. On the other, sunlight flickered through ranks of tall trees, their branches far above her head. Somewhere, an unseen animal gave a sudden, shrieking cry. Elsie jerked with shock, half-turned, and saw John making his way through the trees, heading for a meadow that lay beyond.

She hurried after him, one hand clasped to her head to keep her leaf hat in place.

'Hey!'

The ground was littered with dead branches, making her swerve and stumble. '*Hey!*' she called again, louder than before. Something snagged her leg. She tried to pull free, lost her balance and tumbled into the meadow face-first.

'What on *earth*?' John came striding up, his knobbly knees parting the grass. Elsie got to her feet and straightened her hat. 'I meant to do that,' she said.

'Fathead.'

'*Fathead*?' she repeated. It was obviously meant to be an insult. Elsie glared at him. Uncle John had been much nicer when he'd been old, she decided.

'Go home.'

'You go home.'

'Are you a parrot or something?'

Elsie was trying to come up with a suitable reply, when John froze. His eyes had left her face and were focused on a point somewhere to her left, towards the centre of the meadow. Slowly she turned her head.

'*Don't move.*'

A tiger was standing there, quite still. It was so close that Elsie could have thrown a stone, and – despite her far-from-perfect aim – had a good chance of hitting it. The first thing she thought was how enormous its head was. The second was that even though she had always known the colour of tigers, she had never, up until this moment, realised just how bright, how impossibly orange they actually were.

But she didn't have time to fully register any of this. John's left hand was reaching for the gun at his shoulder. She saw his fingers curl around the trigger, the barrel trembling slightly as it rose.

Ten

The tiger ought to have seen them well before they saw him. He ought to have been able – had he wanted – to come within an arm's length of them, hidden in his own striped shadow, betrayed by nothing but a brief shiver of grass. Instead he had simply walked into the meadow, moving in the way of all tigers, each massive paw placed outer-edge first, each step a decision. The weight of his long body shifting as easily as ocean swell.

But there was a hesitancy to his progress, a strange looseness in his limbs. Something had happened to the tiger that he could not understand. He paced uneasily with lowered head and flattened ears. It wasn't simply that he'd left his territory. It seemed as if he'd strayed from something even more important than that. A kind of path.

He had been born on this path and had walked it all his life. It was the path of greatest advantage, where his feet fell the softest, and the cover was greatest, and the light tricked every eye but his. Never wider than the length of his whiskers, never louder than the snapping of a twig. The unrelenting path of the hunter who knows he is also the hunted.

Now he stood as though lost, his mind blunted by confusion.

Something had happened.

The tiger remembered only snatches. The dawn air full of the cries of men, a hammering of feet, the long grass beaten to a storm. He twisted, crouching to meet the threat, teeth bared.

Then a stinging at his neck, and the ground shifting as if turned to swamp. Weakness seized him. He toppled and lay flat, felt the tremor of approaching steps. A shadow crossed his body. It smelled of something he had never come across before; a bitter, ashy scent, deep-laid and sickly stale. The tiger knew it was the smell of death.

He rolled, caught the ground and bounded clear. He ran.

He ran through a tunnel of fear, never reaching the light, the trees blurring and changing shape, until his hind legs buckled beneath him. He snarled and hauled himself forward, vast shoulders straining, the snap and crash of branches a dim roar in his head.

He was slipping, falling headlong into empty space. Water carried him.

Daylight. He lay high up on the bank, under thin cover, his eyes fixed on a figure at the river's edge. It sat with its back to him, the size of a monkey, hunched like a monkey too, the same intent angle of the head. The tiger felt no hunger, he was too dazed for that. But his mind briefly cleared with a relief so strong it was almost gratitude.

This he knew. *This.*

The intent crouch, and the locked gaze. The inching advance. Each step the sum of a thousand calculations leading to a single, deadly point.

He blinked and pulled back his head. He was mistaken. It was not—

He heard a shrill cry. A stone struck his side, and he staggered, terrified by his own loss of balance. He wheeled and tumbled down the riverbank, clawing at the spinning sky.

He swam, his huge paws beating beneath him, making for the opposite bank, and scrambled out, water sheeting off his back. Then he set off, his pace dogged, yet aimless, his senses dulled. He had been walking like this for several hours when he finally arrived at the meadow.

Now he paused, uncertain of direction, and swung his head slowly around. Catching – too late – the movement in the corner of his eye.

Eleven

'*S*top!' Elsie shouted, shoving John as hard as she could with both hands.

Several things happened, but in such quick succession that they seemed instantaneous. All Elsie registered was noise. John crying out as he fell, the gun going off, the flap and scream of birds. She covered her ears with her hands, her eyes squeezed tight.

When she opened them, the meadow was empty.

'It's gone,' she said.

'Of course it's bloody gone,' John said, his voice jagged. He was still on the ground, struggling to get up. The colour had drained from his face.

'Oh no,' Elsie said. 'Oh no.'

There was blood all over his leg. His sock was sodden with it.

'You've been shot...'

'I can see that.'

'Don't!' He was tugging at the sticky top of his sock, cautiously unrolling it, his breath hissing.

'Does it hurt?'

'What do *you* think?'

She was meant to be Kelsie Corvette. Kelsie Corvette could do first aid in her sleep.

'We have to dig the bullet out. With a knife, or something.'

'Idiot.'

He peered at his bloody shin. 'It just grazed the skin, that's all.'

'Are you sure?'

He didn't answer, either in too much pain, or too angry to speak. Probably both, Elsie thought. She had only been trying to help. And she *had* helped, although he wouldn't ever know it. She had stopped him from killing the tiger.

'You'll have to go home,' she said. 'Do you think you can walk?'

'I'm not going *home*.' He rummaged clumsily in his bag, pulled out a scrap of faded blue fabric.

His hands were shaking.

'I'm not going back without that tiger.'

'You *can't*.'

He began wrapping the scarf around his leg, wincing as he pulled the layers tight and knotted the ends together.

'I'll be fine, all I need to do is rest a bit,' he said, not looking at her.

'But it's gone, it must be miles away by now.'

'Good job I know how to track, then, isn't it?'

He flexed his knee cautiously.

'What if it's worse than a graze? What if it gets infected or something?'

'I told you before, I'm not going back without that tiger.'

Elsie stared at him helplessly. She had forgotten how stubborn her Uncle John could be.

Twelve

They had been walking for nearly half an hour, and every ten minutes, John had looked back at her and said the same thing.

'Go away.'

Each time she stopped a few paces behind, gazing at him in awkward silence until he gave up and continued his lurching, stiff-legged progress.

Elsie was desperate not to lose sight of him. Up until then, she had been too surprised by the events of the day to feel much fear. But with every sweaty step she took, the alarming reality of her situation had grown clearer. She was somewhere in India, in the middle of a forest, with no idea how she had got there, or how to get back, or even if there was an anywhere to get back to. Everyone occasionally lost track of time, Elsie thought, but not *seventy-four whole years*.

Stopping Uncle John from shooting the tiger was beginning to seem the least of her problems.

They had set off in the direction where the tiger had disappeared. The meadow was wider than it first seemed; a sea of tawny grass, dotted with vast, spreading trees, and it was a while before John reached the other side. He stopped at the far line of trees and spent a while hobbling to and fro, staring at the ground and frowning.

Elsie suspected that he had no idea what to do next. At last, with the air of someone who would rather make a random decision than no decision at all, he plunged through an opening in the bushes.

Elsie found herself in a thicket of bamboo, the dense clumps rising higher than a house. It was so quiet she could hear all the ways it was *not* quiet. The whistle of birds, the shifting of leaves, the rustle and tap of a hundred tiny movements taking place just out of sight. She picked up her pace, glancing nervously this way and that.

A movement low to the ground, a rich blue gleam.

'Is that a… *peacock*?' she said out loud.

John carried on walking, as if he hadn't heard, following the path of a narrow, dried-up riverbed before turning abruptly into the forest again.

Something heavy shook the branches of a tree and a twig hit Elsie on the head. She gasped. There were monkeys directly above, five or six at least, with sweeping tails and boldly inquisitive faces. One was tearing at something with its teeth, smacking its lips as it stared at her.

'Wait,' she begged John. '*Please…*'

He stopped, still with his back to her, and she hurried up. There was a moment of silence while he stared at the ground.

'I don't want you here,' he said at last, sounding resigned.

'I know,' Elsie said humbly.

They were standing in a glade, sunlight pouring through an opening in the trees. 'I suppose we could take a short rest,' he said.

He sat down on a fallen branch, grimacing as

he positioned his hurt leg. The scarf had dried to a rusty brown. Elsie hesitated, then sat beside him.

'Bloody stupid outfit for the jungle,' he said, gesturing at her jeans. 'Why're they rolled up like that?'

'Everyone wears them that way in England,' Elsie said. 'It's the fashion.'

'Also, they make good pockets,' she added, reaching into one of the turn-ups and pulling out a flattened package.

'What's that?'

'It's a protein bar,' Elsie said. 'I forgot I had it, until now.'

It occurred to her that protein bars might not have been invented yet. John stared in fascination as she ripped it open.

'What's *that*?'

'The wrapper?' Elsie stuffed it hastily into her pocket. She wasn't sure about protein bars, but she was a hundred per cent certain there was no such thing as foil-lined plastic wrapping. 'It's nothing...'

She carefully broke the bar in half and handed John his share. They sat chewing in silence. John pulled a round, metal water canister from his bag and passed it to her. She took a mouthful and passed it back.

'Why do you want to shoot that tiger so badly?' she said.

'Look, I know you feel sorry for him but he's a man-eater. He was down by the river this morning, near the village. The *dhobi* – the laundry man – told me. They drove him off with stones. He was stalking one of the children.'

'Oh.'

'They don't stop, you know, man-eaters,' John told her. 'They go on killing people until they die, or somebody shoots them. They *have* to be shot, even Mandeep says that's true.'

'Mandeep,' Elsie repeated, remembering the name. Uncle John's friend.

'He said there was one up north that killed more than two hundred and twenty people before it was shot.'

'That's terrible.'

'They're usually old tigers, or ones that've been hurt.'

'The one back there didn't look old or hurt,' Elsie said.

'What do *you* know?' John said, biting his lip. 'If you think you're going to talk me out of anything, you're wrong.'

'Okay,' Elsie said.

'I saw monkeys!' she told him, to change the subject. 'They were looking down at me.'

'Langurs. You'll get used to them. They're everywhere, common as anything. They'll snatch food right out of your hand if they get the chance. Mother hates them, they give her the jitters.'

Elsie thought of the stiff-looking figures in Uncle John's photograph.

'Won't your parents be worried? Do they always let you go off by yourself?'

He shrugged. 'I can pretty much do what I want in the hols.'

'Lucky.'

'My father's in the army. What does your father do?'

Elsie opened her mouth to tell him that her dad was a project manager for an educational software company. Then she closed it again.

'He's sort of like a supervisor,' she said.

'I expect he's ICS,' John said. 'Indian Civil Service,' he added, seeing her blank look.

'Yes, that's right,' Elsie said.

'You'll be for it when they find you've wandered off.'

'They won't mind,' she said. 'I'm allowed to do anything I want too.'

'No, you're not. You're a girl.'

'That's *really* sexist,' Elsie said, outraged.

John looked startled. His face flushed. 'I say, does everyone in England... talk that way?'

'What way?'

His flush deepened.

'I wasn't talking about *that*! Don't you know what "sexist" means?'

He stared at the ground without answering. Even the back of his neck had gone red. Elsie sighed. A lot had happened in seventy-four years.

'Never mind,' she said.

Thirteen

*N*ow that he had accepted the fact that he was stuck with Elsie, John had clearly decided that he ought to look after her.

'You'll need to wear this,' he said, handing her his solar topee.

'But it's yours.'

'I'm more used to the sun than you are.'

The solar topee was too big for her, and rather clammy on the inside, but she took it gratefully. John helped her adjust the strap under her chin.

'That ought to do it.'

'What about your leg? Doesn't it hurt?'

'Can't feel a thing,' he said, staggering to his feet.

They continued on their way, moving slowly, John stopping every few moments to eagerly point things out. 'The black bird over there is called a drongo,' he told her. 'Those webs were made by funnel spiders... that's a mahua tree... and that white one's a ghost tree.'

'A ghost tree?'

'It glows in the moonlight,' John said.

Looking more carefully at her surroundings, Elsie could see that she'd been wrong to think of it as a forest. But it wasn't a jungle either. It was a mixture of the two. Except for the meadows, which didn't seem to belong in either forest *or* jungle but in the English countryside instead...

A flock of lime green birds crossed the sky.

'Parakeets,' John said. 'The ones making all the noise are babblers, awfully chatty things.'

'I wonder what species that is,' he said, gazing at a plant with spiky leaves. 'I haven't seen that kind before.'

A look of deep thought had taken over his face. Elsie knew that expression. For the first time, she could see that he really *was* her Great-Uncle John. The boy standing beside her and the old man in the greenhouse were a single person. Time would change him, and time would leave him just the same.

'You know a lot,' she said.

'Mandeep taught me. He knows pretty much everything.'

'Where does he live?'

'At the house, of course. In the servants' quarters. His mother was my *ayah*; she looked after both of us when we were little.'

'*Ayah*?' Elsie repeated.

John stopped and gave her a disbelieving look. 'You really don't know anything, do you? An *ayah* is like a nanny. Ours has been with the family for years. She looks after my baby sister. She took care of my older brother too, before he went off to school.'

'I didn't know you have a brother,' Elsie said, before she remembered she wasn't supposed to know anything at all about her great-uncle.

'Had a brother,' John corrected. 'He died. Six months ago.'

Elsie gazed at him anxiously from under the brim of the solar topee.

'Horse threw him.'

'That's awful.'

'It was a freak accident,' John said. 'Hugh was a brilliant rider. Brilliant at pretty much everything, as a matter of fact. The headmaster took me out of maths class to give me the news.'

'That's awful,' Elsie repeated.

'Not so bad for me,' John said in the same angry, matter-of-fact way he'd said, 'just grazed the skin' about his hurt leg. 'I didn't really know him that well. He was a lot older, already finished with school. My parents are pretty cut up about it, of course.'

'Yes, they must be.'

They carried on for a while in silence. The trees had thinned, and they were crossing an area of dry earth, dotted with scrubby bushes.

John put a sudden, warning hand on her arm. 'Snake.'

Elsie saw a zigzag movement in the dust in front of her, a gleam of gold and black. '*Oh!*' she cried, shuddering back.

'Banded krait. You have to watch out for them, they're lethal. But they usually leave you alone.'

'Usually?'

'Don't worry,' John said. 'I have a lot of experience around snakes.'

The encounter seemed to have cheered him up. He began to tell her a long story about the time he'd found a viper in his bath. It had been at school. His school was in the mountains; he could see Mount Everest from the top of a hill behind the town. The school term lasted nine months, although it felt like nine hundred because there were so many rules. Everyone counted the days until they could go home for the holidays…

Once he relaxed, Uncle John was almost as chatty as the babblers, Elsie thought. Even his hurt leg seemed better. He was hardly limping at all. She was beginning to hope that he had forgotten about the tiger when he stopped short, peering at the ground. They had come to the edge of a waterhole, its surface emerald with algae. A narrow gully led away to the left.

'I knew it!' John exclaimed.

He pointed to a print in the mud by the water's edge. Elsie saw the shape of a pad, twice as wide as her palm, the marks of four toes around it.

'Know anything about tracking?'

'Yes,' she said. 'Loads.'

'You're looking at it upside down!'

'How do you know it's... the man-eating tiger? It could be a completely different one.'

'The size, for one thing,' John said. 'It's huge.'

'Could be other big tigers in the area,' Elsie said, glancing apprehensively around.

'Not ones that leave prints like that,' John told her. 'Most tigers walk with their claws sheathed. This one has a claw sticking out, same as the pugmarks I saw this morning.'

He didn't have to sound so smug, Elsie thought.

John gripped the strap of his gun, his scrawny neck stretched out as he peered into the mouth of the gully.

'Obviously went into that *nullah*,' he announced.

Elsie stared at the steep, rocky sides of the gully, and the undergrowth covering the floor. 'You're not going to follow it in there,' she protested. 'You could run right into it.'

'Are you saying I'm chicken?' John's voice was fierce.

The Time Traveller and the Tiger

'No, 'course not,' Elsie said, although she couldn't help thinking that he looked rather like a chicken – a plucked one – all bones and pale skin.

'I'd follow it in there,' John said, his voice even fiercer. 'I'd follow it in there if I wasn't with a *girl*.'

Very convenient! Elsie almost said.

'Probably best to take the higher ground anyway,' John commented, narrowing his eyes with an air of great wisdom. 'Ideally, you want to be on the same level when you shoot a tiger. But a shot from above is almost as good.'

Elsie gave him a sceptical look. 'How many tigers have you actually shot?'

'How many have *you* shot?'

'There aren't any tigers in England.'

A maddeningly superior expression crossed his face. 'Didn't think so,' he said.

Elsie wanted to hit him.

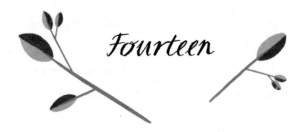

Fourteen

*F*our miles away, on the other side of the river, Mandeep was making his way home. He had been on the move all day, and most of the previous night, although he didn't feel tired. He felt too many other things for that.

Elation at the success of his plan. Alarm at his own daring.

He had never done anything like it before, although he'd thought about it. But then, he thought about a lot of things.

'Always thinking!' his mother said, managing in that way of hers, to sound both disapproving and pleased at the same time. 'Always wandering off somewhere.'

If his mother knew what he'd done, she would

never let him out of her sight again for fear of the trouble he might bring.

His mother worked for the Lassiters. His father too, as head gardener. And even though Mandeep felt fairly sure that the Lassiters had never met the hunter with the glasses and the brand-new jeep, that wouldn't matter.

Mandeep's cousin had told him about it the day before. The hunter had been in the neighbourhood for a while, driving from one village to the next, making enquiries. He was after a leopard, he said. He would pay good money to whoever found him one, provided he wasn't sent on some tomfool, wild goose chase. And it needed to be a healthy animal, not a mangy thing past its prime.

Mandeep's cousin had sold the man a goat to use as bait.

Mandeep had thought about the hunter and the goat all that day, as he helped his father in the garden. It was light work, fetching and carrying, raking the fallen leaves from the lawn.

In the past, his duties had included accompanying John's mother as she collected blooms for the house.

It had been their routine. She in her old gardening hat and floral dress, pruning shears in one hand. Mandeep a few steps behind, carrying the basket for the cut flowers.

'Hold it steady,' she would remind him, as his mind wandered. 'You're tilting it again.'

And then she would place another rose, or dahlia stem, or yellow lily in the basket, and they would move on.

Even after the death of her son, Hugh, the routine had stayed the same. The same basket, the same string of pearls around her neck, the same way she squinted up at the sky, as if bewildered by the sun.

Yet it seemed she walked slower than before, and each day that passed, she walked slower still. Hesitating ever longer beside each shrub and flowering bush. Mandeep's mind could wander across the river, and through the forest, and all the way up to the far northern hills, in the space of time between the opening and closing of her shears.

One morning, about to cut a pale pink, budding rose, she paused for so long that Mandeep grew concerned. His eyes sought the figure of his father, on the other side of the garden. Mandeep was about to call out to him, when she turned, her arm falling to her side.

'I don't think I'm in the mood for cutting flowers today, Mandeep.'

She had not been in the mood for it ever since. Nor for the pruning of the oleander, or the thinning out of the hibiscus and azalea. She didn't even like it when the lawn was cut. The neglect upset Mandeep's father deeply. He was proud of his garden. Yet there was no reasoning with her. She sat for hours in the living room, hardly moving, John's father too. Their chairs positioned on either side of the mantelpiece, with the silver-framed photograph of Hugh in his school uniform placed in the middle.

Mandeep imagined them sitting there until the garden inched over the verandah and up to the door, and the trees pressed dark against the windows of the house, and trails of nasturtium and clematis began to creep across the rug.

But that day, he mostly thought about the hunter and the goat. And when his chores were done, and the evening meal was over, he was still thinking about them. He waited until everyone was asleep, and then stole out of the house, moving quickly, before he could change his mind.

It was nearly a full moon, light enough to see the jeep tracks in the dusty road across the river from the village. But Mandeep didn't need to follow them. He already knew where the hunter was. He knew every acre of these twenty miles of forest, the clearings and waterholes and groves of ancient sal and banyan trees, the crisscrossing paths of its many animals. He'd been exploring it all his thirteen years, sometimes with John, but mostly on his own.

'Always wandering off!' his mother cried, furious because he should be working, instead of wasting time in the forest. But even while she was scolding, she was already forgiving him. And away he would go again.

Some way up the road, just before it curved west, Mandeep saw the parked jeep. From here, the hunter had proceeded on foot, a guide following behind, carrying the heavy gear. They had headed north, skirting the densest areas of trees, making for a place where the ground widened into a clearing with a tall, broad-branched tree in the centre.

Mandeep covered the distance quickly and easily, only slowing as he grew close. He heard a noise and stopped. The noise came again.

The lost baby-bleat of a goat.

Moving with infinite care, Mandeep dropped to the ground and wriggled on his stomach through a maze of strangler vines and thick bushes towards the edge of the clearing. The cool of night had brought out the sweet, woody scent of the trees, mingled with grass and wild basil. A thorn caught his jacket and he paused to unhook himself, sweating despite the chilly air.

He reached the clearing and raised himself on to his elbows to look. The tree was directly opposite. Mandeep could see a *machan* – a wooden platform – wedged between a couple of the lower branches, and the shadowy silhouettes of the hunter and the guide seated on top.

The goat was a milky shape in the moonlight. It was standing in the open, between the tree and the edge of the clearing, a rope tethering it in place.

Mandeep followed the rope with his eyes

without turning his head. He knew the hunter must be looking in his direction, his gun ready, alive to the slightest movement.

The rope ended at a wooden stake buried in a clump of grass near to where Mandeep was lying. He shifted forward, holding his breath, acutely aware of the extraordinary danger of his position. It wasn't merely that he could be mistaken for a leopard and shot at any moment. There was also the fact of the leopard itself. If it was in the vicinity – and Mandeep felt sure that it was – it would have heard the frantic bleating of the goat, just as he had.

There was no way of knowing how close it might be.

From the *machan* came a faint chink of glass. The hunter was drinking to pass the time and keep his courage up.

It would do nothing for his judgement – or his aim, Mandeep thought. But he took the opportunity to scramble the rest of the distance to the wooden stake. It had been driven deep into the earth. Too deep to pull free without a struggle. He groped for the knife at his waist and, shielding the glint of the

blade, began cutting through the rope, keeping the movement restricted to his wrist.

The goat bleated suddenly. Mandeep jerked with alarm, then found his breath and continued cutting. Two more strokes, three.

The rope parted.

Mandeep rested his forehead against the ground for a few seconds, his eyes closed. The goat bleated again, softer than before. He looked up. It was still standing there, foolish in the moonlight. As he watched, it bent its head and began to crop.

Mandeep stared at it in frustration. Then his hand crept over the ground, searching. A pebble, neither too large nor too small. He wedged it tight between his finger and thumb and flicked it as hard as he could. It struck the goat in the middle of its back, and the animal instantly sprang away, crying in panic as it plunged headlong into the undergrowth.

Mandeep heard a muttered curse, the sound of heavy feet descending the ladder from the *machan*. He shoved the knife into his waistband and crawled backwards through the bushes until he could get to his feet and run.

Ten minutes later, he was half a mile away.

It would take the hunter many minutes of crashing through the trees before he recovered his goat. The leopard would be long gone by then. And it would not return in a hurry. With luck, it would leave the area for a while, and the hunter could perch on his *machan* and whistle 'God Save the King', for all the good it would do him.

Mandeep took satisfaction in the thought. The man had no right to go around killing leopards. It wasn't *his* forest.

He spent the rest of the night wedged comfortably in the crook of a tree. And next morning, being in no particular hurry, he took his time making his way home.

Mandeep loved the forest. There was nobody to tell him he was wasting time or scold him for thinking too much. He was free to dream. And perhaps he was more his father's son than he liked to think, because for as long as he could remember, he had dreamed the same thing.

Of the forest as a garden, with a place for everything, and where every living thing was safe.

Fifteen

*T*he tiger had drunk deeply at the waterhole, lapping the golden surface of his own reflection. Then he'd turned and entered the *nullah*, searching for shelter. The water had helped restore him, but there was still a vague buzzing in his ears, as though a swarm of insects were nesting in his brain. He shook his head in a hopeless effort to dislodge them, then slipped into a shadow between the rocks, and lay still.

Sometime later, he heard human voices just beyond, and footsteps advancing above his head. He growled, feeling the sound travel through the ground beneath him. The steps faded away. He slept.

He slept without dreaming, utterly still except for the occasional twitch of his barred tail, and the stir of his breath. The pattern on his body was unique to him, as individual as a fingerprint, his stripes spreading from a central bar along his spine like branches of a blackened tree caught in a forest blaze. His head was marked too, the stripes across his brow unusually thick, giving his face a burned, charred look. They made the white above his eyes and at his throat stand out all the more in the shadowed gloom of his resting place.

When he woke, the buzzing in his ears was gone. He bared his teeth, yawned, and felt his strength return in an elastic rush.

He was hundreds of pounds in weight, yet he could jump triple his own height from a standing position and bring down an animal three times his size. Nothing on earth was faster than his strike. He could swim for miles, see in the dark, and drag the carcass of a buffalo through the thickest of forests. Even his tongue was barbed.

But his greatest strength lay in his ability to think.

The tiger knew how to use the light and the shifting wind to his advantage, how to plan and execute a hundred different methods of attack. His kind had once ranged across half the planet, living everywhere from watery swamps to arctic wilderness. They adapted, they remembered, they *learned*.

Now the tiger rose and shook himself, and paced to the mouth of the *nullah*, every fibre in his body alive to the slightest movement, each step anticipating the one to follow. His eyes burned liquid gold. From the instant of waking, a single thought had filled his mind, stronger than fear, more implacable than hunger.

Rage.

His kind no longer roamed freely. Now their heads were stuck on walls, and their bodies lay skinned and stuffed and pickled. Even their bones were powdered and sold by the gram. A hundred years of murder had shrunk the tiger's world to a fraction of its former glory.

Yet the tiger had no way of knowing this. The cause of his rage was simpler, and much closer to home. His kingdom had been invaded. It was a ruined palace in the mountains, some fifty miles to the north and miles upriver. It had been abandoned for many years, its marble colonnades and graceful arches left for the forest to devour. But its high elevation provided excellent vantage, and there was shade and cover for the tiger among the tumbled columns, a reliable supply of water in the ancient stone cistern.

This was the place from which he'd been driven; sent tumbling head over tail in humiliation. The place where *he* was master.

It could not be tolerated.

The tiger skirted the waterhole, his body a black-slashed rectangle of muscle, his great, scorched head swinging from side to side as he walked. Then, moving with extraordinary power and sense of purpose, he disappeared into the trees on the far side.

Sixteen

The real Kelsie Corvette would not be in this situation, Elsie thought, as she plodded along, her arms grazed by thorns and itchy with insect bites. The real Kelsie Corvette would have everything under control, because the real Kelsie Corvette would not have gone time travelling in an old jumper and T-shirt with one measly protein bar in the turn-up of her jeans.

She would have worn one of those jackets with a lot of pockets. And each pocket would have had something useful in it. Like insect repellent, Elsie decided, scratching her elbow frantically. And binoculars, and a nifty little battery-operated fan...

She glanced anxiously at John. The back of his shirt was so damp with sweat she could see his shoulder blades. He was walking stiffly, his head down.

'Are you sure we're... going in the right direction?' she asked. It had been nearly two hours since they'd left the waterhole and started to follow the gully from above. Almost at once, they'd found themselves in an area so thick with the impenetrable, crisscrossing stalks of dead bamboo that they'd been forced to make a wide detour. John claimed he still knew exactly where the gully was, but after skirting a meadow dotted with sand-coloured termite mounds, scrambling up a rocky slope and making their way through at least a mile of trees, Elsie wasn't confident that this was still the case.

'Of course I'm sure,' John said, not looking up.

'Okay,' Elsie said.

She had seen many more langur monkeys, as well as groups of deer with white spotted backs which John said were called *chital*, and a stork wading in a muddy pool. Now she stopped abruptly in front of a huge web spun between the trees. Something the size of her fist was sitting right in the middle.

'Giant wood spider,' John said in a cross voice. 'Perfectly harmless. You don't have to be a baby about it.'

One good thing about being short, Elsie decided with a gulp; at least she could walk underneath enormous spider webs without getting caught...

But the real Kelsie Corvette would not be thinking this. She would've sorted everything out and be back eating breakfast with Great-Uncle John by now. Elsie hadn't sorted anything out. Yet she hadn't completely failed either. She'd managed to stop John from shooting anything other than his own leg, and she was still keeping up with him, despite being hot and itchy and tired.

Elsie didn't know how she'd found herself seventy-four years in the past, but perhaps there was a reason for it. Perhaps she'd been *sent*. On a kind of mission. To save the tiger. Or save John. Or save both of them. Which meant once the mission was accomplished, she'd be sent back again. That was how it worked, wasn't it? Elsie very much wanted to believe this was true, because the alternative was terrible. If her arrival in 1946 was nothing but a random accident, she might never get back. She would have to live for seventy-four whole years just to catch up to her own time again.

She'd be so old, Elsie thought, that by then she'd probably be dead.

'Are you *sure* we're going in the right direction?'

'I said so, didn't I?'

He stopped and peered at the sun. 'It's this way,' he announced, plunging off to his right.

'Okay.'

All she had to do, Elsie thought, was stick with John until he stopped following the tiger, and then she'd be able to go back to where she came from. In the meantime, she cheered herself up by imagining everything in Kelsie Corvette's jacket pockets.

A penknife with at least twenty different blades and tools, a pair of sunglasses, a first aid kit, a guide to the wild animals of India, a GPS device…

Would a GPS device work in 1946? Elsie wasn't sure, although it seemed unlikely. She had a vague idea you needed satellites for GPS. Well, if she didn't manage to get back to her own time, at least she'd get rich and famous by inventing all the things she knew were in the future. Like satellites and the internet, and video games and microwave ovens, and those chairs that massaged your back, although they were kind of uncomfortable, as well as being creepy...

But you couldn't invent something from the future unless you knew how it actually worked in the first place. Elsie had no idea how a light switch operated, let alone the internet. It probably wouldn't make any difference that she'd come from the future, she thought sadly. She'd have to wait for all the interesting stuff to happen, along with everyone else.

She might have travelled to the year 1946, but she was still the same person who'd found the words, *'Cell' is spelled with a c̲ NOT an s!* written at the top of her latest science homework.

Meanwhile, she had another, far more urgent problem.

'I need to stop for a minute,' she told John.

'Why?'

'I just do.'

'Why?'

'I have to go behind a tree...'

'Oh,' John said, going red again.

Kelsie Corvette would definitely have had a roll

of toilet paper in one of her pockets, Elsie thought, rather wretchedly. Although she'd probably not have needed it in the first place. Going to the toilet was not something main characters did, as a general rule.

She emerged from behind the tree, feeling embarrassed.

'It's okay, you can turn around now,' she told John.

'Are you sure?'

'I just said so, didn't I?'

They carried on, although before long, Elsie stopped once again.

'Do those termite mounds look familiar?' she asked. 'Don't they look like the same—'

'All termite mounds look the same,' John snapped. 'They're *mounds.* All right?'

Elsie didn't want to argue the point, but she couldn't help noticing that the hill to their left looked suspiciously familiar too. And barely five minutes later, there could be no doubt.

They were back at the waterhole, right where they'd started.

Elsie was not the sort of person

who ever said, 'I told you so'. And if she had been, the look of total defeat on John's face would have stopped her. He sat down on a rock, his knees about his ears, his rifle trailing in the dust.

'At least we can fill your canister,' Elsie said.

'Can't,' John said, his head low. 'It'll make you sick as a dog. Water's only good if it's flowing, like a stream.'

'Well, we can splash our faces, can't we? That's better than nothing.'

Elsie went to the edge and looked at the green, soupy water. She was about to lean down and cautiously dip her fingers, when something caught her eye. A shape in the muddy gravel at her feet. She stepped back, still staring.

'It's another print,' she told John.

He shrugged wearily.

'Actually, it's more than one print,' Elsie said, her hands suddenly clammy. She rubbed them on her jeans. 'I really think you need to look at this…'

When John saw what she was pointing at, his eyes widened.

'That's the tiger's print, isn't it?' Elsie said. 'And

that other print, that's one of ours.'

'It's mine,' John said.

'The tiger was here before us,' Elsie said. 'We saw its prints, so how come…'

She didn't need to finish the question. She could tell from John's face that he knew exactly what she was going to say.

So how come the tiger's prints are right on top of ours?

Seventeen

'It must have doubled back,' John said. 'Got behind us.'

'Do you think it could be… *following us?*'

'I don't know,' John said, his knuckles white on the strap of his gun. 'I don't know.'

At once, Elsie realised an obvious, yet terrifying truth; it is one thing to be hunting a tiger, quite another when a tiger is hunting *you*.

She had seen a tiger in a zoo once. It was walking along a path that ran down the side of its enclosure, next to the fence. It must have walked that path ten thousand times before, because the grass was completely worn away. When it got to the end, it turned and came back down again, heading directly towards Elsie at the other side, pacing slowly, as if it carried the boredom of the whole world on its tawny shoulders. It reached the edge of the fence and turned once more, moving like water around a bend in a river.

Elsie had known it would turn. There was nowhere else for it to go. A steel fence and a thick sheet of glass stood between her and the tiger. But for a split-second, as she gazed at that massive form, it seemed as if the opposite would happen. That neither fence nor glass, nor any power on earth could stand in the tiger's way. It would simply keep coming; terrible and unstoppable.

As though it belonged to a world beyond all rules.

Elsie stared at John, her heart shrivelling to a tiny knot in her chest.

'What are we going to do?' she whispered.

He swallowed, his throat contracting.

'We have to go back,' Elsie said. 'We have to go back *now*.'

He nodded.

'At least we know the way,' Elsie said, still whispering. 'All we have to do is retrace our steps.'

He nodded again, then seemed to collect himself.

'No,' he said. 'It's no use losing our heads and simply charging off. We have to *think*. What direction is the wind coming from?'

Elsie tried to concentrate.

'I don't think it's coming from anywhere,' she said at last. 'It's just still.'

'It can't be,' John said. 'The air's always moving a bit.' He licked the tip of his finger and held it up uncertainly.

'Mandeep told me how tigers hunt. They keep upwind.'

'Why?'

'So their prey doesn't catch their scent. Tigers usually attack from behind, so the worst thing you can do is walk in the direction the wind is coming from.'

'Why not walk in the opposite direction, then?'

'Because the tiger could circle around and wait to ambush you downwind. If that happened, you'd meet it head on.'

'So what are you meant to do?' Elsie's mouth had gone so dry that it was hard to get the words out.

'Our best bet is to keep the wind either to the

right or the left of us,' John said, nodding rapidly as if trying to convince himself. 'Right now, I'm pretty sure it's coming from over there, so we can't take the direct route back home. We'll have to zigzag a bit.'

'If we do that, will the tiger give up?'

'Of course not,' John said. 'But it'll have to attack from the side.'

'What difference will that make?'

John slid the rifle off his shoulder and held it ready. 'We'll have a sporting chance of seeing it coming,' he said.

Elsie wasn't exactly sure what a 'sporting chance' consisted of, but whatever it was, it didn't sound nearly enough.

At least he didn't say 'no chance at all', she thought. But it was useless. For once, even she couldn't make the best of it. She took off her hat and tried to wipe her clammy forehead. John said the tiger was a man-eater. He would have shot it in the clearing, only she'd stopped him. And now the tiger was hunting them. Elsie felt sick. She should have known. You weren't meant to change the past. That was the first rule of time travel. You never knew the trouble you might cause.

'Ready to go?' John said.

Elsie squeezed her eyes shut for a second, as if trying to will herself seventy-four years and several thousand miles away. Then she replaced the solar topee and took a deep breath.

'I'm ready.'

Eighteen

Mandeep sat on top of a hill eating the last of the chapatis he'd brought from home and observing the movements of three *dhole* – wild dogs – in the meadow below. After weighing up the pros and cons, he had finally decided that if he could choose to be any animal in the forest, he would be a *dhole*. There was simply nothing about them he didn't admire. Their red coats and neat, high-stepping gait, their playfulness and discipline. The way they whistled to each other, working in formation, loyal unto death to their pack…

He finished eating and shook his bag. Two tiny twists of paper fell out along with the chapati crumbs. Firecrackers. They must have been lying in the bottom of the bag ever since Diwali, a month ago. Mandeep smiled as he tucked them into the pocket of his jacket, remembering the sweets and the flickering candles, the boom and stutter of fireworks above the town, his four-year-old sister, beside herself with excitement, running in little circles, screaming and grinning and covering her ears all at the same time.

A beetle appeared on a rock beside him, trundling slowly over the pitted surface. Mandeep bent his head for a better look. He was fond of beetles. There were so many kinds, all different shapes and sizes and colours, from huge, horned creatures lumbering along, to specks no bigger than a grain of rice. This one was about the size and shape of an almond, with black legs and a green iridescent shell, bright as a jewel.

Mandeep placed his hand and let the beetle walk across the back of it. Its wing cases were like the doors of a tiny, richly crafted box, he thought. A box beautiful enough to hold a treasure. He watched it crawl over one hand and then the other, trying not to think of how angry his father must be at his long absence. There was bound to be trouble when he got home.

Something glinted in the corner of his eye. Mandeep lifted his gaze across the meadow to the line of trees on the far side. The glint came again. He nudged the beetle off his hand and stood up.

A figure was moving among the shadows of the trees. It was the hunter. Mandeep knew because the glint was coming from his glasses, catching the light when he turned his head.

He was walking slowly, yet purposefully. Hunting, Mandeep thought. He must have left his guide and set off alone. What was he after? Not the leopard, that was long gone. Something else, then. Something big. A trophy to make him feel his outing hadn't been a complete failure.

Mandeep didn't think the hunter was the kind of person who liked to come back empty-handed.

He reached for his bag and slung it over his shoulder. Then, acting on impulse, he began making his way down the hill, taking care to keep out of sight as he followed the man below.

Nineteen

*T*he terrible thing about being tracked by a tiger, Elsie thought, was how it made you want to run and freeze at exactly the same time. She settled on taking short, pattering steps that felt as if she was hurrying, even though she wasn't moving very fast at all. Every few paces, she stumbled against a root or tuft of grass, although she didn't dare to look down to see where she was going. She was too busy glancing left and right, her attention riveted on every twitching leaf and shadow. Her neck prickled. She wished her eyes could swivel like a lizard's, so she could look to the rear as well as to the side.

They had set off at a diagonal from the route home, John pausing every few minutes to test the air. He walked ahead of her, taking the lead to give him a better chance of a clear shot if the tiger appeared. After about a quarter of a mile, they entered a thick band of trees. The sun flickered through the trunks, making Elsie blink and rub her eyes.

'Shouldn't we stay out in the open?' she said, her voice trembling slightly.

John didn't answer.

They carried on, passing beneath huge banyan trees that blocked the light. Their branches were so interlocked and tangled that it was impossible to tell where one tree ended and another began. But the strangest things about them were the roots growing from the branches, descending to the earth in hundreds of long, snaky columns.

It looked as if the trees were trying to pull themselves out of the ground, Elsie thought. She almost wished they would. If she had to choose between being chased by a gigantic, runaway tree or a tiger, she'd take the tree. At least she'd be able to see it coming.

'John?' she whispered.

He stopped and tested the air, his body rigid. Then he turned sharply, making for a break in the trees.

Elsie felt certain he had no idea what he was doing, but she decided to say nothing. It helped to have someone in control of the situation, even if they were only pretending to be. The alternative was panic.

They were out of the trees, among low palm bushes, the ground sloping slightly. Elsie's skin was almost raw from the chafing of her jeans, although she realised she could barely feel it. She didn't feel tired any longer either. Or even thirsty. She was far too frightened for that.

John must be feeling the same way. He'd been limping badly during their futile trek from the waterhole and back, but now he was moving as if there was nothing wrong with his leg at all.

When would the tiger attack? What was it waiting for? Elsie didn't know how long she could keep putting one foot in front of the other. She began to hum, very quietly, to keep her courage up.

She was good at humming. She'd had a lot of practice in the school choir.

'*Mmm-mmm-m-m, keep on the sunny, m-m-m-mmm-mm, always on the sunny...*'

'Be quiet. I'm trying to listen.'

'For what? The tiger?'

'No, we haven't got a hope of hearing *that*. But if the deer spot it, they'll sound the alarm call, the langurs will too. It'll give us some warning.'

Elsie heard a whoop in the trees.

'Was that the alarm call?'

'No.'

Something screeched to her left.

'Was that it?'

'*No.*'

'I'm only asking…'

'Well, don't!'

'Okay,' Elsie whispered.

They had arrived at another meadow, and she suddenly noticed that the sun was far lower in the sky than before; light falling in a golden haze over the top of the tall grass. They had been walking for longer than she'd thought. But there was no sign of the track where she'd first met John. Elsie hesitated.

'Are we close, do you think?'

'Pretty close.'

'Are you *sure*?'

'I said so, didn't I?'

Just then, a breeze picked up. For two or three seconds, Elsie didn't pay any attention to it. Then she whirled around.

'It's on my face! It's not coming from the side, it's on my face!'

How long had they been walking into the wind without knowing it? Long enough for the tiger to creep up behind them. For all she knew, it might be there, crouched in the bamboo thicket, only a few paces away.

Elsie stared frantically, saw the bamboo shake. Something was emerging from the shadows. Panic seized her. Running was a bad idea. Running was the worst thing in the world to do. Yet suddenly she was running.

'Hey!' John shouted. 'It's not…'

Elsie didn't hear the end of his sentence. She was already far into the meadow, the solar topee flying off her head as she charged, her heart pounding so hard she couldn't think or see. Grass whipped at her face, yet she carried on, staggering and stumbling until she ran out of breath. She stood still, her chest heaving, waiting for the end.

'Fathead!' John said, stamping through the grass behind her.

Elsie was panting too hard to reply.

'It was only a wild pig. You ran away from a pig!'

'Well, you...' Elsie gasped. 'You said you knew where the wind was coming from, and you *didn't*.'

'At least I was trying to use my head,' John said furiously, 'not walking along chattering and humming like a—'

If he calls me fathead one more time, I'll kick his leg, Elsie thought. Then she remembered she couldn't, because his leg had been shot, and only a truly evil person would kick someone who was already shot. The thought steadied her.

'I don't think the tiger can be following us,' she said. 'Maybe it was for a bit, but not any more. If it was, it would have attacked by now, wouldn't it?'

John was carrying the solar topee that she'd lost during her flight. He gazed down at it, as if examining every detail of the fabric.

'It could have attacked us, and it didn't,' Elsie

persisted. 'Which means we don't have to keep zigzagging and thinking about the wind. We can take the direct route back instead.'

John turned the solar topee around in his hands, apparently fascinated by the row of stitching on the brim.

Elsie stared at him. 'You don't know how to get back, do you?'

There was a new chill in the breeze, and in the distance, something barked with a sound part-wail, part-howl.

'We're completely lost, aren't we?' Elsie said.

John's head jerked up. 'It's all your fault!' he burst out, as if he couldn't control himself for a second longer. 'If it wasn't for you, I'd be home by now, I'd have bagged it, I'd be—'

He broke off, his fists clenched.

'You've spoiled everything!'

'I didn't mean to,' Elsie said. 'I was only—'

'Wherever you came from, you can jolly well go back again,' John shouted. 'On your own.'

'Where are you going?' Elsie said. 'Wait!'

But he had already turned his back on her and

was pushing his way through the grass, his body shaking with rage. A few seconds later he had vanished from sight.

Elsie stood for a moment, staring at the spot where he had disappeared.

'John?'

The sound of barking came again, although this time it seemed a great deal closer.

'John!'

Elsie caught a glimpse of him moving rapidly towards the trees. She hurried after, managing to keep him in sight for a moment or two. Then the grass became so tall that she couldn't see anything at all. She pushed onwards, batting frantically at the stalks, the white feathery tips stirred to a froth above her head.

'John!' she called, her voice smothered by the sound of the grass.

She shouldn't have blamed him for not knowing where the wind was coming from. It wasn't fair of her. She'd *known* he hadn't known. And it wasn't as if she'd had a better suggestion. She'd simply followed along, letting him take the responsibility.

She couldn't have behaved less like Kelsie Corvette if she'd tried.

And now she was lost. Double lost.

'*JOHN!*'

She could be going in circles, for all she knew, although the grass looked thinner up ahead. Elsie rushed towards the opening. She hadn't been going in circles, the trees were right there.

Something strange was happening. The trees were shaking, she could hear the sound of snapping wood, a thundering in the ground. A shape appeared, so sudden and so vast, it was as if the earth itself had risen.

There was no time to turn, or cry out, or even breathe. The elephant was coming straight for her, swinging its trunk as it charged.

Twenty

Despite his shiny jeep and air of self-importance, it seemed the hunter wasn't much of a hunter after all. His progress was erratic, and twice he sat down to wipe his face and stare wearily at his boots. More importantly, from Mandeep's point of view, he seemed totally unaware he was being followed.

A tiger would find him easy prey indeed, Mandeep thought, although the man was in no real danger. Tigers were too wise to attack humans, and too good-tempered to be easily provoked. They rarely showed themselves. Even Mandeep didn't spot them often. He had only met one face to face.

It had happened on a trail. Mandeep had turned a bend and there it was. A tigress walking directly towards him, not ten steps away. They had stopped in surprise and stared at one another. It lasted less than a minute, yet Mandeep could remember every detail. The shudder of her great forepaws in the dust, the lift of her head. Her eyes. The silence.

He'd stood as though turned to stone, transfixed by joy and terror. Then the tigress turned off the trail and vanished into the green.

Mandeep knew that old or wounded tigers could be a menace, hanging around villages, killing cattle, and sometimes even people. They were no trouble in the forest, however, as long as they were left alone.

Yet, of course, they were never left alone.

There was a photograph hanging in the lobby of Mr Lassiter's club in town. Mandeep had seen it six months before. It was the day that Hugh had died. The telephone at the house wasn't working, and Mandeep had been sent to the club to fetch Mr Lassiter home. He had run all the way, and then waited in the lobby while someone went to find him. That was where he'd seen the photograph, hanging between a pair of mounted blackbuck heads.

An old picture. Men with guns. The bodies of tigers heaped waist-high. Twenty tigers, maybe more. Maybe as many as thirty…

'What is it?' Mr Lassiter was there, hurrying across the lobby. 'Has there been an accident?'

Mandeep jerked his eyes away from the photograph.

'What is it?' Mr. Lassiter repeated.

Mandeep couldn't bring himself to answer. But he didn't need to. Mr Lassiter could tell something terrible had happened.

Mandeep would never forget the expression on his face as he stood there, with the ceiling fan slowly turning, the picture of the dead tigers on the wall behind him.

The hunter had crashed his way through a tangled thicket and disappeared from sight over a ridge. Mandeep wasn't particularly concerned. It was becoming obvious that without a guide to help him, the man had little chance of finding anything substantial to shoot. Mandeep was wondering whether there was any point in continuing to follow him at all, when he came over the ridge and saw him in the clearing below. He was lying on his belly, the barrel of his gun resting on a large rock, his gaze intent.

Mandeep raised his head to see what he was looking at.

A male *gaur* – an Indian bison – stood less than a stone's throw away, grazing on the far side of the clearing, and even for a *gaur*, it was enormous. A black, muscled cliff of an animal, seeming far too heavy for its own legs, with a head built like a fortress and curving horns. It had left its herd, as male *gaurs* did from time to time, and there were no animals around to sound a warning.

The hunter had got lucky.

The *gaur* chewed steadily, a look of peace on its mild, bovine face.

If the hunter had his way, that face would soon be staring, glass-eyed, on a very different scene. It would be mounted on a wall, framed by the shadows of its horns, cobwebs gathering around its dusty ears…

The image was so clear and so disturbing that Mandeep lost all sense of caution. His hand shot to his jacket pocket.

BANG!

The firecracker hit the rock to the left of the hunter, the tiny twist of gunpowder exploding on contact.

The *gaur* veered and bolted into the trees, moving with surprising speed for such a hefty creature. Mandeep heard the hunter shout but couldn't make out the words. He was too busy retreating down the ridge, half-running, half-sliding in a tumble of earth and stones.

He picked himself up and sprinted, bent double, through a tunnel of bamboo bushes until he reached the edge of a steep ditch. He leaped into it at once, heading for the shelter of the undergrowth.

There he lay panting, listening for sounds of being followed.

The hunter must have seen him, why would he have shouted otherwise? Perhaps it had been no more than a glimpse, but Mandeep couldn't count on that. The man might recognise him if he saw him again. He might come to the house making enquiries, demanding answers from Mandeep's parents. Mandeep imagined the alarm on his mother's face, and his fists tightened.

But getting angry wouldn't help. He had to *think*.

Staying out another night would worry his parents terribly, although getting caught by the hunter would be even worse. He needed to lie low. He decided to remain in the forest and not return home until the coast was clear.

Twenty-one

The elephant halted thirty paces away in an angry haze of dust. Elsie heard herself whimper, a tiny, rusty hinge of a sound in the back of her throat. She wanted to run, but her legs wouldn't move. Nothing in her body could move.

The elephant made a screaming noise, and swung his head, and took another couple of colossal steps forward.

Elsie covered her head with her hands.

'Don't show fear. Face him down.'

Elsie shot a terrified glance to her right. It was John. He had come back.

'Face him down,' he repeated. His voice was calm, almost conversational. 'That's it. Shoulders square, don't look away.'

'What if it tra... tra... tramples me?' Elsie squeaked.

'Keep your voice nice and low. As if we were just chatting about the weather.'

John came towards her slowly.

'Nothing to see here, old chap,' he told the elephant. 'Nothing at all. False alarm.'

The elephant stamped the ground and then paused, as though weighing up the situation.

'If he senses weakness, he'll try to take advantage,' John told Elsie in the same steady, conversational voice. 'You disturbed him, that's all.'

Elsie took a shaky breath. 'Are you sure?'

'Positive. Look, he's turning away already. Don't take your eyes off him until he's gone.'

They stood side by side, watching as the elephant retreated in a dignified fashion, pausing every few seconds to give them a suspicious look over its shoulder, before disappearing among the trees.

'Best not to hang around,' John said. 'Elephants can be jolly peevish when they've got the wind up.'

Elsie didn't really understand what that meant, but she got the general meaning.

'Thank you for coming back,' she said as they walked swiftly away. 'You saved me.'

John looked embarrassed. 'Quite all right.'

'Sorry for saying that stuff before.'

'Quite all right,' John repeated, looking even more embarrassed.

'What are we going to do?'

'No chance of getting back tonight,' John said. 'We'll have to camp.' He squinted at the sun, and Elsie was glad to see his old expression had returned. As if he was giving the world the benefit of his deepest, most serious thought.

'It'll be dark soon,' he said. 'We need to find a good spot.'

They found one almost immediately, a grassy area on the bank of a rocky stream, the water running golden in the setting sun. John bent and filled his canister.

The moment she quenched her thirst, Elsie realised how hungry she was. She thought longingly of the protein bar.

'Have you got anything to eat?'

John shook his head. 'I might have time to find

something. Know how to build a fire?'

''Course I do.'

'Ever used a flint as a lighter?'

'Loads of times,' Elsie said.

John took his gun and disappeared into the darkening forest.

Elsie stared at the small metal object he had handed her. She had no idea how it worked. She had never made a fire before, let alone used a flint. She had never even been camping, unless trying to spend the night in a tent in her friend Matilda's back garden counted as camping. Elsie suspected it did not. Matilda was so paranoid about snails getting into her sleeping bag, she'd insisted on returning to the house after barely an hour.

Elsie put the flint in her pocket and began collecting stones to put around the fire and a big pile of sticks. She would work the rest out later. It had grown cold, the sky almost empty of light. She paused to pull on her jumper.

A gun fired in the distance. She froze for a second and then hurried to finish her task, her hands shaking.

By the time John returned it was completely dark.

'Gosh!' he said. 'I didn't think you'd manage it as quickly as that!'

Elsie sat beside the crackling fire, feeling pleased with herself.

John was looking equally triumphant. 'I shot a jungle fowl!' He held it up.

'So, you got the hang of the flint,' he added. 'Well done!'

Elsie hesitated, struggling with herself. But it was no use.

'I found a box of matches in my jeans,' she confessed. 'I must have tucked them in there when—'

She was about to say *when I was lighting your stove this morning*, but she stopped herself in time.

'I also found some paper,' she said. 'That helped to get it going.'

Her worksheet from the school trip to the wildlife centre more than a week ago. Her class had been doing a project about ecosystems. Elsie had no idea why she'd folded up the sheet and stuffed it into one of her turn-ups. For the same reason she'd put the matches there, she supposed. Just out of habit.

'Poor thing,' she said, gazing at the bird dangling from John's fist.

'We're hungry, aren't we?'

Elsie nodded.

'Mandeep says that jungle fowl are the ancestors of all the chickens in the world.'

He kneeled down and began plucking the feathers from the bird, biting his lip with concentration.

'How do you know how to do that?'

'I've watched the cook enough times,' John said.

They roasted the meat on a skewer made from a twig, and while they waited for it to cook, they refilled the canister, and brewed tea with a handful of loose leaves which John brought out of his bag, wrapped in a scrap of newspaper. The jungle fowl was raw on the inside, and burned on the outside, but perfectly cooked in between, and they ate it greedily, without pausing to talk, or even wipe their mouths.

Elsie thought it was the most delicious meal she had ever eaten.

When they were finished, they boiled another

canister of water and attended to John's leg. The scarf was stuck to his skin with blood, and it took a lot of careful dabbing before Elsie could finally unwrap it, doing as best she could by the light of the fire. John sat still, his eyes squeezed tight.

'Does it hurt?'

'Can't feel a thing,' he said, gasping slightly.

But once the scarf was off and the wound thoroughly washed, and he could examine the damage for himself, his body relaxed. The furrow on his shin was long, yet shallow. The bullet had only scored the skin.

'Told you it was just a graze.'

'We still have to bandage it up again,' Elsie said. 'You don't have a pair of scissors, do you?' she added, after a moment's thought.

'My penknife has scissors. They're pretty crumby, though.'

'Can you close your eyes?'

'Why?'

'Just do it.'

He did as she asked, although Elsie still retreated to a safe distance, beyond the circle of firelight, before removing her jeans. He was right, the scissors *were* pretty crumby, she thought, as she began hacking at her turn-ups. It didn't help that it was almost pitch dark and there might be any number of wild animals lurking nearby. Elsie paused and stared uneasily around her. Her heart bounded.

Two shadowy, caped figures were standing beneath the trees.

'Who... are you?' she gasped. Then she saw that it was only a pair of termite mounds.

'I knew that's all you were,' she whispered. 'You can't fool *me*.'

It took a lot of stabbing and ripping, but at last the turn-ups were cut away. Her jeans felt strangely light once she'd put them back on.

'I've got you a bandage,' she said, returning to the fire.

John didn't answer.

'Aren't you even going to look?'

'You didn't tell me I could open my eyes!' John said.

Elsie sighed. 'Well, you can. *Obviously.*'

Having been kept safely rolled, the fabric in the turn-ups was still relatively clean. Elsie made a long strip of it and wound it around John's leg.

'Better?'

He nodded. 'No use keeping *this*, though,' he said, picking up his blood-stiffened sock. He hesitated, and then threw it on the fire.

They sat for a while without talking, watching as the flames found the woollen shape and devoured it with a satisfying hiss. It was a clear night, with more stars than Elsie had ever seen before. The forest was quiet; a watchful, living kind of silence, filled with a million unheard things. Deep in the darkness, an animal yelped with a wailing, mewing sound.

'Jackal,' John said.

'Are we… safe out here?'

'Pretty safe. With the fire.'

Elsie inched closer to the warmth. 'I don't know how it can be so cold. It was hot during the day…'

'Just wait till the summer. Heat's awful, makes you ill. And then there's the monsoon.'

'Is that why you have to go away to school for most of the year?'

'Suppose so.'

'Don't you get homesick?'

John jabbed at the fire with a stick, sending up a shower of sparks. 'No use making a fuss about it,' he muttered. 'Everyone's in the same boat, you know.

'I say,' he added, quickly changing the subject, 'I don't suppose you thought you'd be spending the night in the jungle when you got up this morning.'

'No,' Elsie agreed. 'I didn't.'

'When did you arrive anyway?'

Elsie wasn't sure how to answer this. She could hardly say, 'I've only been here a day,' because then John would wonder how she had managed to wander so far in such a short space of time.

'Um, yesterday?'

John whistled. 'Well, that explains a lot. Don't worry,' he said kindly. 'You'll soon get the hang of the place. Is your house in town?'

'Yes.'

'I wonder if my father knows your father,' John said. 'Does he go to the club?'

'Yes,' Elsie repeated, reverting to her tactic of agreeing with everything.

'They probably know each other, then. Probably old friends.'

'Probably…'

'Just yesterday,' John said, marvelling. 'Well, you'll be able to write a jolly interesting letter to your friends back in England about your first day in India!'

There was such camaraderie in his voice as he sat there, the firelight playing over his thin, earnest face, that Elsie suddenly wanted to tell him everything. Where she had really come from, the open greenhouse door, the strange scent of the blue lily in its ancient pot. The way he'd said, 'You can't go wrong with bacon!' as he heaped her plate. How it felt to know something impossible: that even though she was sitting right there beside him, it would be ages and ages before she was actually born.

She couldn't. He would think she was completely insane.

'Back when… we were arguing,' she said, 'you shouted that I'd spoiled everything. Why?'

John gazed at the fire, studying the embers. His shoulder gave a little twitch, as if he'd been about to shrug and then changed his mind.

'The tiger, I suppose.'

'I stopped you shooting it, but why does that spoil everything?'

'It's a man-eater.'

Elsie wished she hadn't brought it up. He looked so angry, all his friendliness gone.

'It's a *man-eater*,' John repeated.

Not angry, she realised. More as though he was about to cry.

'I would have shot it, and then I'd have got it home and everyone would have seen,' he said.

'Seen what?'

John didn't answer. He sat hugging his knees, his eyes still locked on the fire.

'Hugh was good at everything,' he said at last.

'Your brother?'

'He was all my parents cared about. Now he's dead. And he's still all my parents care about.'

It was Elsie's turn to be silent. She knew what it felt like to be overlooked.

'I wanted to do something… amazing,' John said.

Elsie nodded.

'Just for once,' John said, his voice bleak. 'I would have been...'

A main character, Elsie thought.

'You saved me from the elephant,' she pointed out.

John shook his head. 'I gave you some good advice. Anyone could've done that.'

Elsie wanted to tell him that when he grew up, he would become a doctor and help people get well – perhaps even save their lives. But she had a feeling that even if he believed her, it wouldn't count. He would probably think being a doctor was giving 'good advice' too.

'Well, I think you were really, really brave,' she told him.

'What rot,' he said, although Elsie could tell he was pleased by the way he rushed to change the subject.

'We should dig a hole for what's left of that jungle fowl and build up the fire. Get some sleep.'

'You mean, just lie on the ground?'

'Where else? You can cover yourself with some of those dead leaves.'

'Not even take off our shoes?'

'Best to keep them on. You don't want to wake up in the morning and find a couple of scorpions hiding inside, do you?'

Elsie wished he hadn't mentioned scorpions. She lay down facing the fire, her body tightly curled. Nobody could rest like that, she thought. On the ground, under a scratchy blanket of dead leaves, with scorpions running around trying to get into her shoes. It was impossible.

Twenty seconds later, she was fast asleep.

Twenty-two

The night brought weight to the forest, turning the meadows and groves into solid blocks of darkness. Only the tiger was immune. The denser the shade, the more insubstantial he seemed to become, until he was as grey as smoke and almost as transparent.

He had been on the move for most of that afternoon, walking steadily, with an unhurried, undulating pace, pausing every few minutes to turn his head in the direction of some sound, before going on his way. Out in the open like that, stark against the green foliage, he was impossible to miss. Yet he was built to vanish when he chose, the outline of his body splintering among the grass, his stripes dissolving into shadow, each back paw placed exactly where the front had been, to leave the fewest prints.

He paced on, slipping between patches of cover, his eyes wary. He was in unknown land here, a threat to any other tiger whose territory he crossed. And territory was all. A tiger fought to gain it and must fight to keep it, as long as his strength held. He needed fifty pounds of meat a week merely to stay alive, and fearsome though he was, might attack many times without success before he made a kill. Territory was precious, ceaselessly patrolled, its borders marked and marked again.

The tiger had come across several such markings in the course of the afternoon. Rocks bore the scent of spray, and high up the trunk of a tree there were deep gashes left by claws. Disquiet grew in the tiger.

Another had walked this way. A female. But the scent was old, and the bark already healing over the claw marks.

In the evening he came to a pool, sunk between boulders, and entered it to rest. He stayed there for a long time, soothed by the water and the cool. Yet he was still far from home and his hunger was growing, a coil in his chest that tightened by the minute.

At last he emerged. The moon which had risen huge and yellow above the trees was smaller now and high in the sky. Night was the best time for hunting, the deer huddled, blinded by the dark. The tiger crossed a thinly wooded clearing and stopped short, his attention caught by an unfamiliar thread in the air; the scent of water and burned wood, the faint, tantalising aroma of meat. He lowered his head and sniffed the ground around a pair of termite mounds. Then he padded forward.

Burning embers. Humans lying still, light playing on the pale ovals of their faces. The tiger gazed at them for a moment. Then the breeze shifted, filling his nostrils with the harsh scent of wood smoke. His nose furrowed into deep grooves of distaste and he turned away, his eyes glowing green in the moonlight.

Twenty-three

It might have been the cold, or the sudden chorus of birds, but Elsie knew differently. It was beauty itself that had woken her.

She opened her eyes to a world turned silver and gold. A bright haze hung over the stream, dazzled by rays of sun and the luminous sheen of water. Everything was shining; the wet stones, the feathery-tipped grasses, the termite mounds glittering with tiny specks of mica. Even the webs of the funnel spiders at the bases of the trees seemed to glow, like scraps of dream left over from the night.

And there, by the edge of the water, stood a deer. It had tiny, pointed hooves and velvet horns and white spots dancing over its back as if it had brushed against the stars.

'*Ohhhhhh*,' Elsie breathed.

The deer lifted its head, listening. Then John shifted on the ground nearby and the deer leaped away, disappearing into the mist with a single bound.

'You scared it off,' Elsie said.

John sat up blearily, leaves sticking to his hair. 'What time is it?'

'I don't know,' she said. 'It's freezing.'

They stood up, shivering and stamping their feet.

'Do you have any tea left?' Elsie asked hopefully.

John shook his head. 'Take too long to get the fire going anyway,' he said, kicking stones over the heap of ashes. 'Nothing to eat for breakfast either. We might as well get going.'

'Maybe we should wait until someone comes to find us,' Elsie suggested. 'Your parents must be looking for you.'

'They've probably sent people out to search,' John said, sounding depressed. 'There'll be a fearful row when I get back.'

They washed their hands and faces in the icy stream, and then took stock of their surroundings.

There was a hill in the distance, with a flat top and relatively few trees growing on its slopes. John stared at it, shading his eyes with his hand.

'Good view from up there. Might be able to get my bearings.'

'But it'll take you ages.'

'Not if I run.'

Elsie remembered her first sight of him, tearing down the path towards her.

'I like running,' he said.

'What about your leg?'

John prodded the denim bandage and flexed his knee a couple of times. 'Feels fine.' He slid the gun off his shoulder and handed it to Elsie.

'If anything attacks you, shoot it,' he said.

'But I don't know how!'

John made a face. For a second Elsie thought he was about to call her a fathead again. But he restrained himself.

'Won't be long.'

Elsie thought he'd been lying about his leg, but as soon as he took off across the clearing, she knew he'd been telling the truth. Nobody could run like that if they were badly hurt. She stared after him in amazement.

It wasn't just that he was fast. It was the way he ran. Effortlessly, all his awkwardness gone. As if his skinny body suddenly made sense.

As if running was what he was meant for.

He reached the edge of the clearing, disappeared into a thin band of scrub, then emerged and began making his way up the slope to the summit of the hill, still moving at what seemed like incredible speed.

Fifteen minutes later he was back. Elsie knew because she'd been counting. Which meant that it was probably a lot less than fifteen minutes, because she always counted too fast. It was probably more like ten. And that was with an injured leg. Elsie looked down at her dusty trainers.

An injured leg and no proper running shoes.

They hadn't been invented yet.

John leaned from the waist, panting, his face bright.

'You're really good at running,' Elsie told him. 'Really, *really* good.'

'I know where we are!' John said, his breath still

coming hard. 'Or how to get back, at least. I saw the river.'

All they had to do was follow it, he explained. It would lead them to the village. From there, his house was no more than a mile away. As soon as they arrived, his father would contact her parents and they would come and pick her up.

'They must be going crackers,' John said, 'wondering where you are.'

'Yes, they must,' Elsie said, looking down at the ground.

Twenty-four

They set off in the direction of the river, John walking confidently ahead while Elsie lagged behind. She couldn't help worrying about what was going to happen next. If she didn't find a way to get back to her own time pretty soon, she'd have to go home with John, and she didn't like that idea at all.

She felt certain his parents would ask a lot more questions than he had done. And Elsie had a feeling that simply saying 'yes' to everything wasn't going to work. Perhaps she could pretend to have lost her memory. If she kept repeating, 'Sorry, can't remember!' they would have to give up, sooner or later…

'Come on,' John called. 'Keep up!'

She heard the rushing of water and hurried

towards it, pushing through thick bushes. The river was wider than she'd imagined, the water brown and swift, swirling around boulders and fallen branches. Elsie looked downstream. From somewhere just out of sight came a roaring, white-water sound.

Rapids, she thought. Big ones.

'It looks deep,' she said.

'Not really,' John said. 'You should see it after the monsoon.'

They were standing close to the water, at a spot where the ground dipped to form a narrow, muddy beach. Further along, the riverbank grew steep again, dense with roots and tumbled rocks. Elsie was about to point this out and suggest it might be easier if they retraced their steps slightly and followed the river from a distance, when John gave a start, and dropped to his heels.

'What are you doing?'

He peered at the ground, his hands on his bony knees.

'It's the same one, I'm sure of it!'

'The same what?' Elsie asked, although she had a sinking feeling that she already knew the answer.

'See the claw mark? It's definitely the same one.'

'It crossed the river,' John said, straightening up. 'Prints leading down to the water, but none going in the other direction. That proves it.'

The wretched tiger, Elsie thought. *Again.*

'They're pretty fresh,' John said. 'It must have passed close to our camp last night.'

'Well, it can't be a man-eater, then, can it?' Elsie said. 'Otherwise it would've eaten us,' she added.

John didn't reply, his eyes scanning the opposite bank. 'I bet I could find the spot where it came out of the water.'

'It doesn't matter. We have to go back to your house, don't we?'

John squatted again. 'Yes, pretty fresh,' he repeated to himself. 'I could pick up the trail on the other side.'

'But we have to go back! You said your parents will be worrying. You've been gone for ages.'

'All the more reason to have something to show for it, then.'

'You can't cross, it's too deep.'

'I've done it before.'

Elsie stared at the fast-flowing water. 'You've crossed it *here*?'

'I need a stick, that's all.' He turned and began rummaging in the bushes, tugging at the knotted branches.

'You mustn't go after that tiger,' Elsie pleaded. 'You *can't*.'

'You said that before.' John was still searching among the bushes. 'I don't know what makes you so sure.'

There was nothing for it, Elsie thought. There was no other way of preventing him. She drew a deep breath.

'I'm sure because you told me. You said killing that tiger was the worst thing you ever did.'

'But I haven't killed it!'

'I know.' Elsie sat down on a rock with an air of resignation. 'I'm from the future,' she said.

'Stop messing around.' He took out his knife and began sawing at a branch.

'I'm not, it's true. I'm from seventy-four years in the future and you're my…'

Elsie paused. She had to explain things to John,

but it probably wasn't a good idea to completely freak him out. 'I was visiting you,' she said in a rush. 'You live in a village in England and after you killed the tiger it was made into a rug and you have it in your spare room and you still feel bad about it.'

'Seventy-four years in the future?' John said. 'I must be jolly old!'

'Yes, you are.'

'Stop talking rot. If you want to get across the river with me, you'll have to find yourself a stick.'

'But it's true!' Elsie cried. 'One minute I was there and the next I was here!' John was staring at her as if she'd gone mad, but she ploughed on, describing the greenhouse and the strange flower, and how she'd told herself she must be dreaming.

'That's why I couldn't tell you where I lived, because I don't live anywhere. My dad isn't friends with your dad. He doesn't even *exist*. Look at my clothes!' Elsie lifted one of her feet. 'These are called "trainers". You've never seen anything like them before, have you? That's because they haven't been invented yet.'

John waited for her to finish, his arms crossed.

'If you come from the future,' he said, 'you must know what's going to happen.'

'What do you mean?'

'In the world. All the stuff that's going to happen.'

'Not all of it,' Elsie protested.

'Well, the main things.'

'Of course I know the *main* things.'

'What are they, then?'

Elsie opened her mouth and then closed it again. What *had* actually happened in the last seventy-four years? History was one of her better subjects at school, but so far, they'd only got up to the Tudors. She racked her brains, trying to recall what her parents talked about when they discussed the news. Wars in far-off places, how dreadful so-and-so was. But she didn't know how to explain any of it.

Then she thought of John's earlier comment about girls. 'Well,' she said, a touch triumphantly. 'You might be interested to know that a woman got to be prime minister ages ago, and then another one did, and women fight in the army and play professional football and run companies and… and all sorts of things.' Elsie stopped, out of breath.

'You expect me to believe that?' John said with unconcealed scorn.

'Also, there's climate change,' Elsie said, beginning to feel desperate. 'That's a big thing. The environment, endangered species, the ocean filling up with plastic…'

'You're talking gibberish,' John said. 'You're throwing out random words.'

Elsie twisted up her face in an effort to think of something – anything – that might convince him.

'I know!' she burst out. 'Men landed on the moon! They walked around and planted a flag.' Elsie remembered seeing the grainy picture on TV. 'It was an American flag.'

'You're telling me America is going to *own* the moon?'

'Because they planted a flag?' Elsie felt confused. 'I don't think it works like that any more…'

'If I was going to pretend to be from the future, I'd come up with much better stuff than that,' John said.

Elsie hesitated. She had remembered something else. Her mother had been talking about it on the drive to Great-Uncle John's house. Elsie had been too busy writing about Kelsie Corvette's latest exploits to pay much attention, although she'd got the basic facts.

It related to John.

Elsie didn't want to upset him, but it might be the only way to make him see she was telling the truth.

'You're going to leave here,' she said, speaking fast to get it over with. 'India, I mean. I don't know when it happens, but I think it's soon. My mum told me about it. The British people left and went back to Britain because the Indians wanted their country back, which was fair enough, really.'

Elsie's mother had also told her that the British had no right being in India in the first place, but Elsie thought it probably wasn't a good time to mention that.

'You'll be allowed to visit,' she continued, in an effort to let him down lightly, 'for holidays and stuff. My friend Matilda went last year. She sent me a photo of the Taj Mahal, only you couldn't really see it because her head was in the way...'

Elsie's voice trailed off. John's shoulders were down, and he was thumping his new stick on the ground, as if to test its strength.

'You don't need to come from the future to know *that*,' he said, still thumping furiously. 'My parents talk about it all the time. Everyone in the whole country knows about it!'

'Oh,' Elsie said, feeling deflated.

'Are you finished jawing?'

'No, I'm not!' Elsie jumped to her feet in agitation. 'I *am* from the future, and loads of things have happened, like the internet, for example, and smartphones. You can do *everything* with a smartphone, like instantly send messages and photos and links and look up stuff, and pay for things, and find your way when you're lost…'

John stopped thumping. 'Interesting,' he said. 'Do you have one?'

'Yes, I do!'

'Where is it, then?'

'I left it behind,' Elsie admitted. 'I wasn't carrying it when—'

'As I thought,' John said. 'I see your game. You

think if you waste enough time telling ridiculous stories you'll be able to distract me. Well, it won't work.'

Elsie shook her head, defeated. What was the point of being from the future if nobody believed a word you said? All she'd done was make John even more determined.

'You coming?' he said.

'It's too dangerous.'

'Nonsense. Waist-deep at worst.'

'*Your* waist, maybe.'

'Suit yourself. If you follow the river, you'll be able to find your way home easily enough.'

He took off his shoes and single sock and looped them round his neck. Then, with solar topee on head, stick in hand, and a look of great resolve upon his face, he stepped into the water.

Twenty-five

Mandeep woke with a feeling of dread. He'd been away from home for two nights now. His parents were used to his disappearances, but even so, they must be getting frantic. It would make them all the angrier when he did return. His father was a quiet man who never raised his voice. Yet Mandeep knew what he would think.

An idle, disobedient boy. Spoiled by his mother.

Mandeep set off, pushing his troubles to the back of his mind. He had found a wild gooseberry tree, and ate the fruit for breakfast as he walked, listening to the secret drip of dew falling from leaf to leaf. The sun rose higher, sending vast columns of light pouring through the ancient, stately trees. It was a sight Mandeep had seen a thousand times before, but it never failed to inspire in him the same hushed awe that he imagined he might feel in the hall of some great temple or the palace of a king.

He wandered slowly, pausing at everything that caught his attention. A trail of ants, the blue flash of a kingfisher, snake tracks in the dust. Every so often, he stopped to examine an item in more detail. A feather dropped by an owl, the tiny white skull of a vole. Mandeep's jacket pockets were full of such treasures. He kept them for a while until new ones took their place. A few were too precious to discard, and these he stored in a special pocket, sewn into his jacket's lining. There was a tiger's canine tooth, and a scale from the armoured back of a pangolin, and a reddish, nut-like seed that Mandeep's grandfather had once given him.

The seed didn't look like much, although his grandfather had held it in the palm of his hand as if it were a ruby.

'Take it. For good luck.'

His grandfather was ill, his mind scattered. He'd told Mandeep things that made no sense. The seed was from the rarest plant in the world, he said. He had seen the flower when he was young. He had seen it just a few years ago.

'What do you mean?'

His grandfather put the seed in Mandeep's hand, curling his own hand around so that Mandeep made a fist. He began to talk again, even more strangely, as if he was half-dreaming.

Mandeep didn't understand, and his grandfather never had a chance to explain his words because he died soon afterwards, so soon that Mandeep was still holding the seed when he went.

That made it a treasure.

Mandeep crossed the river at a spot where the water ran shallow over flat, raised rocks. He climbed a ridge, meandering down the slope on the other side, heading in the direction of home, although he wasn't sure how near he ought to go. It might be prudent to wait until nightfall before approaching the house. Just in case.

As he arrived at the bank of a stream, something caught his eye. The remains of a fire. Mandeep ran the tip of his finger over the ashes. They were thickly layered, it must have burned for several hours.

He stood up and looked around, saw a scattering of sticks and branches, a white scrap pinned beneath. He tugged it free. A sheet of paper, torn in half and heavily creased, as if it had been folded many times. Mandeep smoothed it out on his knee. Near the top he saw a line of text, printed as if in a book. Underneath, someone had added two or three sentences in pencil. He could make out a few phrases: *all linked... everything... or else... will die...* But the writing was so crooked and misspelled that it was difficult to make much sense of it.

He frowned. He was reasonably good at reading English. He had learned it in the village school. But there were words here that he didn't understand. He folded the piece of paper carefully and put it in his bag to study later.

Mandeep didn't think the hunter had made the fire. He was a long way off, probably still on the other side of the river, or else had given up and returned to whatever place he'd come from. Perhaps it was John, although it was unusual for him to be so far from home, and he'd have told Mandeep if he'd been planning an expedition.

Mandeep paused. Maybe not. They usually spent a lot of time together during John's school holidays. This year, however, John had mostly kept to himself. Mandeep might have been hurt by this, although it was inevitable that they should grow apart, sooner or later. But in his heart, he knew John hadn't changed.

He was just unhappy.

Mandeep walked across the clearing, studying the ground. There was a place where the bushes had been pushed aside. He followed in the same direction, moving cautiously, heading towards the river again.

Twenty-six

*E*lsie had no choice. She had to follow John. It was either that or be all by herself.

In the middle of India. In 1946.

There wasn't any time to find a stick, but perhaps she wouldn't need one. Further downstream, there was a big, flat rock in the middle of the river. The water looked slightly shallower there. Elsie decided to keep her trainers on. She might slip with bare feet, and her trainers would dry soon enough.

The water was colder than she'd thought it would be, and after a few steps she was already up to her knees. She could feel the tug of the current, strong enough to knock her off balance unless she was careful. She paused and took another step, pebbles shifting beneath her feet, the white-water sound even louder than it had been before.

She glanced to her left. John was already halfway across. He was up to his waist, holding the gun above his head, his stick planted at an angle, as if the water was trying to pull it away.

It was a good thing she had cut the turn-ups off her jeans, Elsie thought. The weight of all that waterlogged fabric might have been fatal. She was up to her thighs now, although the rock was only a few steps away. A stone slipped against the side of her foot. She lurched forward, almost fell, clutched at the rock just in time and pulled herself up.

She teetered across and looked down. Immediately, her heart sank. The water was far deeper on the other side of the rock. The riverbed had formed a hole there, she couldn't even see the bottom.

'John?' she called.

He was in exactly the same spot as before, only his stick was gone.

'John!'

He swayed, righted himself and took two or three struggling steps, the current rippling against his shirt. He reached a trapped branch sticking out of the water and hooked his gun over the end of it, followed by his bag and his shoes.

He can't carry them, Elsie thought. *He's frightened he'll lose his balance.*

'Stop!' she shrieked. 'Go back!'

John grasped the branch for a moment, as though hesitating. But the opposite bank was tantalisingly close, a few more steps would bring him there. He looked over his shoulder at the way he had come, and back at the bank again. Then he let go of the branch and made a wild lunge for solid ground, as if speed alone might save him.

A second later he was down, the current sweeping him off his feet as effortlessly as if he were a twig. She saw his arms thrashing as he grabbed at the overhanging bushes on the far bank. He caught a leafy strand, held it for a split-second, then lost his grip and was carried away.

Elsie screamed.

There was someone next to her on the rock, she had no idea how or when he had got there. He was crouching low over the edge, his hands reaching for a fast-moving shape. She saw him grip the back of

John's shirt and pull him to the rock. Then she was crouching too, tugging on John's arm as he hauled himself up, coughing and spitting and looking thinner than ever from his drenching.

Elsie stared at John's rescuer. He was about twelve or thirteen, not as tall as John, but stronger-looking, wearing a grubby shirt and jacket with a length of cloth wrapped around his waist like a skirt and a yellow feather sticking out of one of his pockets.

But what struck Elsie most were his eyes. They had a bright intensity, as if the boy was searching the world with his gaze.

'Mandeep!' John gasped. He seized the boy's arm, water dripping down his shocked face. 'You saved my life!'

Twenty-seven

They sat on the riverbank, John still wringing water from his shorts.

'This is Kelsie, by the way,' he told Mandeep. He paused. 'What's your surname again?'

'Corvette.'

'I still think that sounds made-up,' John said.

'It is very good to meet you,' Mandeep said. Elsie liked the careful, almost formal way he spoke English. It made him sound kind.

'But we have not solved the problem of the gun and the shoes,' he said.

'I forgot all about them!' John said. 'Jolly good thing I hung them on that branch. I'd have lost them otherwise. How on earth am I going to get them back?'

Mandeep retrieved a coil of rope from his bag. John could wade into the river tied to the rope, he explained. He would be safer that way.

'It's not long enough,' John said. 'I say we find a forked stick, use that instead.'

If she *had* been Kelsie Corvette, this would have been the perfect moment for her to demonstrate her lassoing skills, Elsie thought sadly. Compared to long-horned bulls, a pair of shoes hanging from a branch would have been child's play.

John and Mandeep were still debating the merits of stick versus rope.

'I'm telling you,' John said.

'And I am telling *you*,' Mandeep replied.

They didn't seem angry. Or even impatient. As if they were so used to arguing that it didn't seem like arguing any more. They were both the same, Elsie thought. Each as stubborn as the other.

No wonder they were friends.

In the end, a compromise was reached. John waded out as far as he could, holding on to the rope, then used a stick to reach the rest of the way, unhooking his possessions with a triumphant flourish.

'Shame about my topee, though,' he remarked. 'Must be five miles downriver by now.'

Elsie produced it from behind her back. While the others had been rescuing John's belongings, she had been pottering among the rocks further downstream. She'd spotted the solar topee bobbing in the shallows and had fished it out with a stick of her own. After removing the river debris and brushing it off, it looked almost as good as new. She handed it over, pleased with herself.

He took it without a word. Elsie felt crushed. Saving someone's hat wasn't nearly as impressive as saving their life, but it was still *something*. He might have thanked her.

He was too busy showing Mandeep the tiger prints in the mud, gesturing to the other side of the river, his face excited.

Mandeep looked down and said something in a different language, his voice low. Elsie didn't know what John said in reply because he began speaking the same language as Mandeep, his words coming fast, as if he was trying to convince him.

Mandeep didn't answer. He stood still, not looking at John.

They were arguing, Elsie thought, although it was different than before.

'What are you saying?' she asked. 'What language are you speaking?'

'Hindi, of course,' John said. 'Mandeep says the tiger didn't kill the child by the river yesterday morning, and *I'm* pointing out that was only because the women surprised it and drove it away.'

He began to speak Hindi again, louder than ever, not seeming to notice that Mandeep was growing quieter and quieter.

Elsie started to think perhaps she didn't like John very much, after all.

'So, it's settled,' he announced. 'We'll go upstream, find a safe place to cross the river, come back down on the other side and pick up the tiger's trail.'

Then he turned and marched off, without giving the others a chance to respond.

They followed in silence, keeping a little way behind. After a couple of minutes, Mandeep fetched a handful of almonds from his bag.

'Would you like some?'

Elsie nodded.

'You can crack them with your teeth,' Mandeep said. 'The shells are not so hard.'

'Okay,' Elsie said, feeling shy. 'Thanks.'

They chewed for a while, not saying anything, gazing at John striding ahead.

'He shouldn't be doing this,' Elsie said at last.

'Once he has made up his mind, it is not an easy job to change it,' Mandeep said.

'But you think it's a bad idea, don't you? You said the tiger hadn't killed that child. It might not be a man-eater at all.'

'Probably not.'

'He's only doing it to try and impress his parents.'

'Yes,' Mandeep agreed. 'Because of Hugh.'

Elsie stared crossly at John. He hadn't turned to look back at them, not even once. 'I don't know why he's being such a *bully*,' she said.

'It is because he knows he is in the wrong,' Mandeep said simply.

John's hair had dried in a funny way, sticking up on the back of his head. Elsie suddenly felt sorry for him. He would have to give up sooner or later. The tiger must be far away by now. She doubted they would even find its tracks. And as it turned out, she was right.

They found something much worse instead.

Twenty-eight

By the time they reached a place where they could safely cross the river, after over an hour of walking, John had slowed enough for the others to catch up, although he still maintained an offended silence. He sat apart while they stopped for a rest and a drink of water, glancing at Elsie and Mandeep when he thought they weren't looking and kicking a loose root in the ground.

Mandeep divided the rest of his almonds and shared them with the others. They ate slowly, trying to stretch out the tiny meal.

'Are you *sure* you don't have any more?' Elsie asked.

John bent his head, staring at the last two nuts in his palm.

'You can have these if you want,' he said abruptly, handing one to Elsie and the other to Mandeep. 'Not terribly hungry, you know,' he added stiffly.

Elsie could tell he wanted to be friends again but wasn't sure how to do it.

They set off once more. Elsie's legs were aching after all the walking she had done the previous day, although it didn't bother her as much as it might have done.

Mandeep had so much information about the forest and was so good at pointing out things she might never have noticed that she forgot she was tired. For a while, she even forgot she wasn't supposed to be here, seventy-four years in the past, and thousands of miles from home.

'Where there are spotted deer, there are always langur monkeys,' Mandeep told her. 'They help each other like a team.'

'Bamboo is a strange plant,' he said. 'It grows for more than thirty years, flowers just once and then it dies.'

'There's another of those huge spiders!' Elsie cried.

'It's a female,' Mandeep told her. 'The male is ten

times smaller and she will eat him if she gets the chance because she is always hungry.'

'That's terrible,' Elsie said, grinning at him. 'What an awful wife to have!'

John was growing more and more miserable as they chatted. He had started to limp again, wiping and re-wiping his face with the back of his hand.

'We must be getting close,' he muttered every few minutes.

Elsie felt certain that he was sick and tired of the search, and was longing to give up but was too proud to admit it. All he needed was an excuse, she thought. A way to save face.

A few moments later, he found it.

A jeep, parked in the middle of a dirt path.

'Hello!' John said eagerly. 'What's this?'

The jeep looked new, despite the dust on its wheels and bonnet. It was empty, apart from a large solar topee lying on the passenger seat. 'Might be someone out looking for us,' John said. 'We'll have to go back with them. What rotten luck.'

'Yes.' Elsie gave him a look. 'Rotten luck...'

'Where's Mandeep?' she said suddenly.

'He was here a minute ago!'

'He vanished,' Elsie said, staring back the way they had come.

A loud, angry shout came from their left, immediately followed by a cry of pain.

'Mandeep!' John darted forward, then stopped short. A man with sandy-coloured hair and glasses came striding out of the trees. Mandeep was with him. The man was holding his arm in a tight grip, jerking him sharply each time he stumbled.

'What the devil are *you* doing here?' he said when he saw John and Elsie. He gave Mandeep's arm another, harder jerk.

'Let him go,' John cried. 'He hasn't done anything.'

'He needs to turn out his pockets first.'

Mandeep didn't move, his face blank with fear.

'He hasn't done anything!' John repeated.

'That remains to be seen.' The man tightened his grip until his fingers were digging into Mandeep's arm. 'Come on! Empty them!'

'You can't just attack him!' Elsie burst out, shocked. 'That's child abuse!'

The man stared at her for a second, as though she'd

gone completely mad, then turned back to Mandeep.

'This is the fellow who's been following me, almost sure of it. Deliberately scaring the game. Deliberately!' His voice rose with fury. He took a breath, smoothing his hair back in place with his free hand, as if trying to gather himself.

'Biggest *gaur* I've ever seen, I had it in my sights. And now I think of it, there was something damn fishy about my missing goat. Rope looked as if it had been cut with a knife.'

The memory seemed to infuriate the man all over again. He jerked Mandeep's arm even harder.

'Stop hurting him!' Elsie cried. 'You can't *do* that!'

Nobody was listening to her. A look of caution had come over John's face. He wiped his hand on his shorts and held it out.

'My name's John Lassiter.'

'Gordon,' the man snapped, ignoring the hand. 'Eric Gordon.'

'I think there must be some mistake, Mr Gordon. Mandeep can't have been following you. He's been with us all day.'

'Ah, but it's yesterday I'm talking about. Where was he yesterday?'

'He was with us yesterday too,' John said. 'We've been tracking a tiger.' But he hesitated for a fraction of a second before telling the lie, and Elsie could tell Mr Gordon didn't believe him.

'I still need to see what's in his jacket.'

Mandeep looked at John, and back at Mr Gordon. Then he removed his jacket silently, with an air of defeat.

'What's all this rubbish?' Mr Gordon said, rummaging through the pockets, and tossing out an assortment of scraps. A look of triumph seized his face. 'I thought so!'

He held up a small twist of paper.

'But it's just a firecracker,' John said.

'Exactly!' Mr Gordon resumed his grip on Mandeep's arm. 'It's all the evidence I need. He's coming with me.'

'I'm sure my father can sort this out,' John said, speaking rapidly. 'I'm *sure* of it.'

Elsie gave John a puzzled look. Why was he talking about his father? Surely it was *Mandeep's* father who ought to be contacted. Then she remembered where she was. Mr Gordon would be far more likely to believe John's father for one simple reason. Because John's father was British. That was how the system worked in this time and place. Elsie stared silently at the ground, her shoulders hunched with discomfort.

'If you could just drive us home…' John begged.

'Impossible, I'm afraid,' Mr Gordon said, when he heard the name of the town. 'That's miles out of my way.'

He began marching Mandeep towards the jeep. Elsie and John hurried after him. 'I have to contact my parents,' John said. 'I *have* to!'

Gordon hesitated, as if registering their bedraggled appearance for the first time. He glanced at John's bandaged leg and single, drooping sock.

'Well, I don't suppose I can leave you out here alone,' he said, his voice grudging. 'You'll have to come along too, sort things out when we get to Sowerby's place.'

They sat in the jeep, Elsie in the middle, staring at the back of Mr Gordon's head as they went along the bumpy track.

'Who *is* he?' Elsie whispered.

'Don't know. Don't know who this Sowerby is either.'

'Do *you* know?' Elsie asked Mandeep.

'I don't know where he came from,' Mandeep muttered. 'Only that he was after a leopard…'

Elsie was still holding the yellow feather from Mandeep's jacket that she'd picked off the ground. She smoothed it out and placed it on his knee.

'Well, I don't care who he is,' she whispered. 'I hate him.'

Twenty-nine

They drove through the forest, slowing to a crawl as they manoeuvred over ridges and across the beds of dried-up rivers, speeding up as they regained the path, the trees flicking past in a blur. Elsie glanced at Mr Gordon's face in the rear-view mirror. His glasses, reflecting the light, were two blank and burning discs. Then he shifted his head a fraction, and she saw his eyes, watching her.

Elsie looked away instantly, her hands tightening in her lap. Perhaps he had noticed the strangeness of her clothes. Perhaps he was wondering where she came from. The thought frightened her. She nudged John.

'Don't tell him I'm from the future,' she whispered.

'I won't,' John whispered back. 'Because you're not.'

'Where are we going?' he asked Mr Gordon.

'I told you, Sowerby's place.'

'But who is he?'

'You mean you haven't heard of him?' Mr Gordon wrestled with the gear stick. The jeep made a grinding noise, earth spraying beneath the wheels. 'Man's famous. Best hunter in India, if not the world. You must have seen pictures of him.'

'Maybe,' John said. 'I don't know.'

'You'd have remembered him if you had,' Mr. Gordon said. 'Imposing-looking chap.'

He could hardly say the same about himself, Elsie thought, with his weaselly features and thin moustache.

'Sowerby's a living legend,' he continued in the same enthusiastic tone. 'Must have bagged pretty much everything on the planet, although tigers are his real speciality.'

Mandeep turned his head towards the window, as though willing himself far away.

'Didn't you say you were after a tiger yourself?' Mr Gordon asked.

John didn't answer.

'What's that? Speak up!'

'Yes,' John muttered.

'Then you're in for a treat, Sowerby's an expert. There's nothing the man doesn't know about tigers. He's so good at tracking them down that it's almost uncanny. If I didn't know better, I'd think he could actually communicate with the brutes. I've been pestering him for ages to let me join one of his hunts.'

'Is that why you're going there now?' Elsie asked, too disgusted to keep quiet. 'For a hunt?'

'For a *tiger* hunt,' he corrected. 'Sowerby holds them once or twice a year. Only for a select few, mind you. He's very choosy about his guests, and rightly so. I've heard the hunts are spectacular. I thought I'd come a day early, get some useful tips from him before the others arrive.'

Elsie didn't reply, although there was a lot she would have liked to say. She pressed her lips together, her heart hammering with indignation.

The conversation about hunting now over, Mr Gordon didn't seem to have anything else to talk about and they continued to drive in silence.

After about an hour on forest tracks, the jeep turned on to a paved road, apparently empty of all other traffic. The brightness of the morning had vanished, and the sun was no more than a smudge in the white, glaring sky.

It was past lunchtime. But Elsie was too nervous to ask Mr Gordon how much longer the journey would take. He kept his eyes on the road ahead, sweat running down the back of his neck to meet the stained ring on the inside of his collar.

After a while, John fell into a doze, his head bobbing with every lurch of the jeep. Elsie looked at Mandeep. Apart from replacing the feather in his jacket pocket, he had barely moved. He sat stiff-backed, his eyes wide and watchful.

The road wound into a long bend, and then another, as if they were going uphill, although the rise was so gradual that Elsie was hardly aware of it. Then the trees cleared for a moment and she caught a glimpse of the horizon, hazy in the distance, the land spreading for miles to meet it. They had climbed much higher than she had guessed.

'Do you know where we are?' she asked Mandeep.

He shook his head tightly. 'I have never been here before. We must be twenty-five miles from the river by now, maybe more.'

They carried on, the road still rising. The jeep slowed and turned on to a narrow track, then again on to an even narrower one. Dense walls of vegetation rose on either side as the jeep pushed onwards. The walls grew higher, until the sky was nothing but a ribbon between. A moment later, it had vanished completely.

They were in a tunnel of such deep green that it was almost black. Elsie could barely see her own hands in the darkness. All she was aware of was the swish and thudding scrape of branches lashing the sides and roof of the jeep. They sounded like claws, she thought. As if she had entered the lair of some terrible beast. For a moment, panic engulfed her. Then the track widened a fraction and they were out of the tunnel. They turned a final bend and stopped.

Thirty

$\mathcal{E}$lsie saw an area of flattened earth dotted here and there with trees. In the middle stood a two-storey building with a broad roof and white wooden pillars framing a long, shady verandah. Five or six smaller buildings were clustered behind, separated by a low stone wall.

Mr Gordon turned off the engine and in the sudden silence, she heard the pulse of the forest surrounding them. Two men wearing white tunics and trousers hurried over and began taking luggage out of the back of the jeep.

Mr Gordon opened the passenger door for them to get out.

'Not you,' he said, putting a heavy hand on Mandeep's shoulder. He said something to one of the men, his voice brusque. The man nodded.

'Come along with me,' Mr Gordon told the others. Elsie didn't want to go, but there didn't seem to be much choice. She followed him up the stairs, on to the verandah, past an arrangement of wicker chairs and tables.

She glanced back. Mandeep was being hustled away, around the side of the building. Elsie tried to see where they were going, but the front door had opened, and she was being ushered through. A stern-faced man in a turban and jacket led them silently across a hall with a coat stand and a collection of walking sticks. John slipped the rifle off his shoulder and carefully propped it in one corner. Then the man opened another door and gestured for them to enter.

They were in a spacious living room, shuttered against the light, filled with comfortable-looking sofas and armchairs, a bookshelf, and several lamps with fringed shades. Bottles stood in a neat line on a bar at one end, and on the wall above the fireplace hung the head of a bear. It was black, with a cone-shaped snout and a bewildered expression, as if it was surprised to find itself there, and was still trying to fathom out exactly what had happened.

'Lord, I need a drink,' Mr Gordon said, throwing himself down on the sofa. 'Whisky,' he told the man in the turban. 'And make it a large one.'

He glanced at Elsie and John. 'I suppose you're hungry. There'll be something or other to eat in the kitchen. The bearer will show you.'

John didn't move. 'I have to telephone my parents.'

Mr Gordon took a gulp of whisky, swallowed it and let out a satisfied sigh.

'A telephone?' he retorted. 'Out here in the middle of nowhere? Not likely!'

'Can someone be sent to fetch my father, then?' John said. 'He'll be worried about us. He can sort everything out when he gets here.'

'I don't know about that. I'm a guest. You'll have to take it up with Sowerby.'

John stared at him helplessly, but he could see it was no use. The bearer was already indicating for them to follow. They went out of the room and down a corridor to the kitchen at the back of the building.

'There's no one here,' Elsie said.

'Don't suppose the cook was expecting us,' John said. 'Lunch must have been over ages ago.'

He was right, the cook hadn't been expecting them. He appeared a few moments later, looking grumpy, and set to work with a great thumping of pots and pans.

John and Elsie sat nervously at the table to wait.

'Did you see where they took Mandeep?' Elsie whispered.

John shook his head, his face anxious.

'What *is* this place?' Elsie asked.

'Hunting lodge, by the look of it.'

'Do you think your parents know you're with Mandeep?'

John nodded. 'They must have guessed, and that means they won't be as worried. But yours must be frantic. They probably think you've been eaten by wolves.'

'They don't think anything,' Elsie said. 'They can't. I told you, they haven't even been born.'

John made a face. 'Don't start *that* again.'

The cook turned around abruptly and placed

two plates of scrambled eggs and toast in front of them. He stood by the table, his arms folded.

Elsie took a cautious bite. The eggs had a strange, soapy taste.

'It's delicious,' John said.

'Yes… *delicious*,' Elsie echoed.

The cook didn't reply, although his grumpy expression relaxed a fraction, and after they were finished with the eggs, he produced dessert, laying it before them with a flourish.

Elsie stared at the wedge of blancmange. It had a flabby, slippery texture, although it didn't taste of anything bad. Instead it tasted of nothing at all, which somehow made it even worse. But she could feel the cook's eyes on her, and she hurried to finish, holding her breath and trying to smile politely at the same time.

'What do we do now?' she asked, after the last slimy morsel had gone and the cook had cleared the plates.

'The only thing we *can* do,' John said. 'Talk to Sowerby.'

Thirty-one

*E*lsie felt better after her meal, despite its peculiarity, although as the bearer led them up the wooden staircase to meet Sowerby, she couldn't avoid a creeping sense of dread. Part of it was not knowing what had happened to Mandeep, and part of it was the unease on John's face. But mostly it was the silence.

No noise came from the outside. All she could hear was the slap of the bearer's shoes on the floorboards and the sigh of the overhead fan, one of its blades slightly crooked, making a *pah-pah* sound as it beat the still air.

They reached the top of the stairs and found themselves on a wide landing, with doors to rooms either side, and a huge, empty space in the middle, surrounded by a wooden railing. Elsie peered over, saw a long table beneath, and guessed she was looking down at the dining room on the floor below.

The bearer stopped at a pair of double doors. He tapped softly, and bent his head, listening. Then he opened the door and they stepped inside.

Elsie's first thought was that it was the most cluttered room she had ever seen. It was so crammed with objects that it was impossible to focus on anything in particular. Yet she had the sense that there was something vaguely wrong about everything there. As if each item – from the ornate pieces of furniture to the hundreds of ornaments crowding every surface – was shaped a little oddly. But she didn't have time to work it out. All her attention was drawn to the man sitting in the centre of the room.

Mr Gordon had described Sowerby as imposing, and now Elsie understood why. At school the previous year, she'd learned about tectonic plates. They lay beneath the surface of the earth's crust and when they shifted, the force of the impact made canyons split and mountains rise. Sowerby had the same look. As if vast, subterranean forces had formed his features, from his jutting chin and stone-slabbed forehead to the high, lonely ridge of his nose.

He stared at the children, although it was impossible to read any expression in his eyes, buried beneath his overhanging brows. All Elsie could see was that they were black and utterly unblinking, despite the grey thread of smoke rising from a cigarette smouldering beside him.

'John Lassiter,' John said, advancing a little uncertainly. 'And this is Kelsie…'

'Corvette,' Elsie muttered, following him.

Beneath her feet she felt an unfamiliar texture. At first glance, she'd thought the floor was covered with rugs. But they weren't rugs. They were animal skins; deer, zebra, lion, leopard and bear; so many that they overlapped, flattened legs spread, as if reaching for each other. Elsie drew a sharp breath. A musky odour filled the air, mingling with the cigarette smoke.

'Gordon tells me he picked up the pair of you on his way here,' Sowerby said. He took a drag on his cigarette, his eyes not leaving John's face, then tapped the ash in a bowl at his elbow. 'Rather far from home, aren't you?'

John nodded.

Sowerby glanced at the window, as if judging the angle of the light.

'One of my men could drive you back, although you'd have to leave immediately,' he said.

Elsie was startled by his rudeness. He wasn't even trying to hide the fact that he wanted them gone. But she didn't care. She suddenly felt desperate to be gone herself. There was something disturbing about Sowerby's chair. It had elephant tusks instead of arms, the ivory stained and worn to a polish where his hands had rested. And she couldn't help noticing that the bowl where he had stubbed out his cigarette wasn't really a bowl at all. It was a lacquered turtle shell, gilded around the rim.

'What about Mandeep?' John said.

'Ah, yes, the Indian boy,' Sowerby said. 'The one who's put Gordon's nose out of joint.'

'But that's just it, sir,' John said. 'There's been a mistake. Mandeep hasn't done anything wrong.'

'That's not what Gordon says.' Sowerby rose from his chair and crossed the room to the desk. 'He tells me the boy sabotaged his hunt. Frankly, he needn't have bothered, since Gordon was unlikely to get anything anyway. The man's completely inept.' Sowerby reached into a box on the desk and took out another cigarette. 'But that's hardly the point, is it?' he said, turning his gaze back on John.

Elsie was aware of John saying something in reply, although she was too distracted to listen. She had suddenly realised why everything in the room looked strange. Sowerby's chair, his ashtray, the twisting legs of the desk, the mottled picture frames, the lampshades, the peculiar ornaments...

They were all made out of animals, or parts of animals.

She hadn't spotted it straight away because a great deal of trouble had gone into making the animal parts look like completely different things. The wastepaper basket was an elephant's foot, the candelabra an assortment of tusks, the lid of a chest the broad back of a crocodile. Zebras had given their legs to chairs and monkeys their paws to dresser handles. The clock ticked in a skull and tails that once whisked flies away now tied the curtains back.

Hundreds of living animals, Elsie thought. *Murdered and turned into stuff.*

'Are you sure of that?' Sowerby was saying.

'Yes,' John said, although there was a catch in his voice. Perhaps the horrible contents of the room were getting to him too.

'I'm afraid it's impossible,' Sowerby said. 'Gordon's determined to keep the boy here until he can turn him over to the authorities. And I'm not inclined to argue with a guest. Not when they're paying me as much as he is.'

The cigarette lighter on Sowerby's desk was made of bone, highly polished and curved to fit the hand. He lit his cigarette with a flick.

'You'll have to go back without him,' he said.

'I can't do that, sir,' John said, with a brave straightening of his shoulders. 'He's a friend, you see. He saved my life.'

'Suit yourself,' Sowerby said.

For a second, Elsie was too outraged to be frightened. 'But you have to let Mandeep leave!' she said, her voice coming out in a squeak. 'You can't just *keep* him!'

Sowerby glanced over, as if noticing her for the first time, then looked away.

'If my father was here and could talk to Mr Gordon, I'm sure he could explain everything,' John said in a rush. 'Can't you send word to him? He could be here in the morning.'

Sowerby's expression didn't change. Elsie wasn't sure it could. But his eyes narrowed for an instant. He shook his wrist and looked down at his watch, then crossed the room and pressed a button by the door.

'It's later than I thought,' he said. 'Too late to send anyone out this evening. We'll discuss it tomorrow. In the meantime, I suggest you get cleaned up and give your clothes to be washed. You'll be shown where everything is.'

John looked upset, as if he wanted to say more, but the bearer had arrived to escort them away, and Sowerby was already closing the door behind him.

Thirty-two

They were shown to a room on the ground floor. The furniture was sparse, the rug was threadbare, and the two beds little more than metal cots. But it was a relief to find themselves alone.

They sat on the beds in silence for a moment or two.

'That room…' Elsie said at last.

'Ghastly.' John's shoulders slumped. 'Good job Mandeep didn't see it. He's potty about animals.'

'Do you think Mr Gordon's right about Mandeep spoiling his hunt?'

'Pretty sure. Unfortunately.'

'I don't care. Mr Gordon's still in the wrong.'

'I'll tell you something else that's wrong,' John said. 'Sowerby didn't mind about us going back, but the minute I asked him to send for my father instead, he suddenly decided it was too late in the day. Did you notice that?'

Elsie nodded.

'Bloody fishy, in my opinion.'

'I don't understand how they can just kidnap Mandeep and talk about taking him away somewhere,' Elsie said. 'He's a *kid*.'

'That probably won't make much difference. There's a lot of unrest – rioting, stuff like that – going on in the country. The newspaper is full of it. My father says it makes people nervous. Mandeep could be in trouble if the authorities think he's an agitator.'

'Just because he's Indian?' Elsie burst out, shocked by the unfairness.

'Yes, of course because of that!'

'You don't have to snap at me.'

'Sorry.' John put his head in his hands.

Elsie's nose itched. She rubbed it, wondering if she was allergic to something. Her friend Matilda would know. Matilda had a lot of allergies, although they mostly came on just before gym class or in the middle of a test...

There was a rattling, pattering sound. Elsie looked out of the window to see where it was coming from. Four or five langur monkeys, their tails curled into hoops, were running across a metal roof to her right. As she watched, others joined them, leaping from the overhanging branches of a nearby tree, one with a baby clinging to its back like a tiny jockey.

'Isn't that the roof of the kitchen?' Elsie said.

John still had his head in his hands. 'It's all my fault,' he said. 'I got Mandeep into this.'

'Not really,' Elsie pointed out. 'He was the one who spoiled Mr Gordon's hunt, so he got himself into it, didn't he? Not that he wasn't *totally* in the right,' she added.

'I don't mean then. I mean at the river. Mandeep didn't want us going after the tiger. He told me that. But I knew I'd get my way, that he wouldn't make a fuss or try to stop me.'

'Why not?'

'Because he's…' John's voice trailed off.

Because he's the gardener's son and his family works for your family, Elsie thought. They might argue about trivial things, but when it really mattered, John always had the advantage, even though Mandeep was supposed to be his best friend. Yet John was too ashamed to admit it. That was why he hadn't been able to finish his sentence.

'If I hadn't been behaving like an ass, we'd never have run into Gordon and we'd all be home by now,' John said, leaping to his feet and pacing across the room in agitation.

'Do you really think your father will be able to sort it out?'

'Not sure he'll get the chance. I had the feeling Sowerby doesn't want him turning up. I bet you anything he'll fob me off with another excuse tomorrow morning.'

'But why?'

John didn't answer. He stopped pacing and sat on the bed again. 'I'll find out where Mandeep's being kept and then I'll wait until night and get him out.'

'I'll help,' Elsie said.

'How?'

Elsie tried to think of something. 'I could hold the torch,' she said at last. 'Because of the dark,' she added, although she could tell she hadn't convinced him. He shook his head.

'Not necessary,' he said with an air of great conviction. 'I've got it all worked out already.'

Thirty-three

The rest of the day passed slowly. While John went off to investigate Mandeep's whereabouts, Elsie crept across the hall to the common room, hoping to distract herself with something to read. She peered around the door, dreading the thought of finding Mr Gordon there, or worse, Sowerby himself. But the room was empty.

There weren't many books on the shelf, and most of them looked like depressing reading. Elsie passed over *Big Game Hunting in Every Continent*, *The Illustrated Guide to Pig-Sticking* and *Taxidermy for Amateurs*, before choosing – in desperation – *The Memoirs of Col. H. Featheringstone-Follerby, Vol. II.*

The book had been written nearly a hundred years ago, judging by the date on the cover. Elsie perched on the edge of the sofa and opened it at random.

The autumn of 1858 found me back in the foothills, keen to resume my long-standing acquaintance with tigers, she read. *The beaters raised a pair on the very first day of the shikar, both of them whoppers. I put two balls from my double Kennedy into the chest of the larger one, turned, and made a very pretty shot into the neck of the second. She gave a tremendous leap into the air, rolled a dozen feet and plunged into the ravine…*

Elsie looked up, caught the baffled gaze of the bear on the wall above the fireplace, and hastily turned the page.

Tigers are cowardly brutes on the whole, although this one was cornered. I pulled the trigger and the gun missed fire! Here was a rum go! I was perfectly cool however and took a second bang at him that dropped him like a stone. It was, I decided, an uncommonly good day's sport…

Elsie couldn't read any more. She closed the book and shoved it back on the shelf, wiping her fingers on her jeans with a sick feeling. Out in the hall, she met John coming in the other direction, looking triumphant.

'I know where he is!' he said, as soon as they were back in their room.

'How did you find out?'

'I asked the cook. He brought Mandeep some food earlier. They're keeping him in an outhouse. It isn't locked, just bolted at the top and bottom.'

'Did you speak to him?'

'Too risky. I stuck a note under the door instead. Told him I'd get him out tonight, as soon as I could.'

'Well done,' Elsie said.

'It was easy,' John said. 'Piece of cake.'

They ate supper alone in the kitchen. The cook had left them a dish of something that John called 'kedgeree'.

'Is it *supposed* to taste of liquorice?' Elsie asked.

John grinned and shook his head.

'Must be his own secret recipe,' he said.

The cook had told John that three more guests were due to arrive the following day and the tiger hunt would take place the day after that.

'We'll be long gone by then,' John said. 'Mandeep

too—' He broke off. 'Are you picking your nose?'

'I'm not! It's itchy!'

'That's what everyone says when they're caught picking their nose.'

'I'm *not!*'

'Have it your own way,' John said, smirking.

There were pyjamas, neatly pressed and folded, laid out on John and Elsie's beds, for after they had taken their baths. Elsie didn't know who the pyjamas belonged to, except that it must be someone much larger than she was. On the way to the bathroom, she got muddled, turned left instead of right, and found herself by the common room. Voices came from behind the door.

'Awfully decent of you to spare me the time.' It was Mr Gordon speaking.

He was getting some hunting tips from Sowerby before the other guests arrived, Elsie thought. On an impulse, she bent and peered through the keyhole. She could see Mr Gordon's feet and knees, his hand curled around a glass of whisky, and opposite, the craggy profile of Sowerby's head.

'Went to one of your lectures, once,' Mr Gordon

was saying. 'You said tigers can communicate using a sound too low for the human ear to make out. Forget the word for it, something scientific.'

'Infrasound,' Sowerby said.

'That's the one. Sounded like a lot of mumbo jumbo. If you can't make out a sound, how d'you know it's there at all?'

Sowerby stretched his lips in an approximation of a smile.

'You can call it infra-something if you like,' Mr Gordon continued. 'But *I* call it having a sixth sense. It's the secret of your success, my dear fellow. It's why you're a legend.'

What a suck-up! Elsie thought.

Just then, Sowerby turned his head and glanced at the door. Before Elsie could move, he was staring straight at her, his eyes boring through the keyhole, as if he could tell she was there. She jerked upright, not daring to make a sound, her face burning.

Perhaps Gordon was right. Perhaps Sowerby really *did* have a sixth sense.

They were talking again, although Elsie had stopped listening. She scurried away, her pyjamas clutched to her chest, heading for the safety of the bathroom.

It was clean, although dimly lit, with a cast iron bath and overhead pipes that gave out a wheezing, whistling sound when she turned on the tap. The water ran scalding hot for a moment or two and then grew rapidly more and more lukewarm, although Elsie didn't mind. It was wonderful to wash after two days tramping through the forest. She took the cracked bar of soap from the dish on the side and scrubbed herself until the bath was lined with grime.

It was absolutely quiet. Even the pipes had fallen silent. Elsie sat with her knees up, staring at the old-fashioned silver taps. But, of course, they weren't really old-fashioned. The future hadn't happened yet.

This wasn't the past. It was Now.

Elsie remembered what she'd said to John about her parents not missing her because they hadn't been born yet. It had comforted her at the time, although now a disturbing thought struck her.

Her parents might not miss her even *after* they'd been born.

If she didn't get back, nobody would miss her. Not her parents, or Matilda, or even Great-Uncle John. They'd never know she was supposed to be there. *The Incredible Adventures of Kelsie Corvette* would never be written. And it wouldn't matter in the least.

It was worse than being an extra in a film, Elsie thought, tears pricking her eyes. It was like being an extra whose scene gets cut before the film ever comes out.

A drop from the tap broke the still surface of the water with a tiny *plop*. Elsie lifted her head and wiped her face. It was no use crying. Any minute now, John would be hammering on the door, wanting to know what she was doing. Elsie scrambled out of the bath and hurriedly dried herself.

The good thing about pyjamas that were far too big, she decided, was that she didn't have to bother with the bottom half. The top made a perfectly fine nightdress all by itself. Elsie was so pleased with this simple solution that she padded back to the bedroom feeling almost cheerful.

'About time!' John said. 'It's a complete mystery

to me why girls take so long in the bathroom.'

'You don't know any girls,' Elsie pointed out.

He spent just as long as she had done, and when he finally returned, Elsie had to struggle to keep from laughing. He'd pulled his pyjamas up as high as they would go and tied the extra fabric in knots on either side of his waist. They made him look like a periscope, she thought, with the knots as handles.

It was late. John went to the window and lowered the blind. He looked at his watch.

'When are you going to get Mandeep out?'

'Best to give it a couple of hours,' John said. He sat on the edge of the bed, his hands clasped and his face resolute. Elsie lay down and stared at the ceiling. Across the cracked surface, two speckled brown geckos crept on sticky feet, hunting for insects. Somewhere in the building a door closed, and footsteps passed overhead with a creaking of floorboards.

John reached for the bedside light and turned it off. 'No need to draw attention to ourselves,' he said.

Elsie wondered uneasily what geckos did in the

darkness. 'I don't like it here,' she whispered. 'It gives me the creeps.'

'Don't be a wet blanket.'

'You don't like it either!'

'True,' he admitted.

'I just thought of something,' Elsie said. 'Do you remember, in the jeep, when Mr Gordon was talking about how hard it is to get invited to one of the hunts here? He said Sowerby was really choosy, didn't he?'

'What about it?'

'But Sowerby told us Mr Gordon's a *terrible* hunter. It doesn't make sense.'

'I'm beginning to think,' John said, 'that there's rather a lot about this place that doesn't make sense.'

Thirty-four

*E*lsie was determined to stay awake to keep John company, but she couldn't stop wondering whether the geckos were anywhere nearby. It might be safer if she took cover. She crawled into her bed and pulled the sheet over her head. In a moment, she was fast asleep.

Three hours later, she woke with a start. Someone had turned the light on. Elsie sat up abruptly, blinking at John in the sudden glare.

'Have you gone already?' she said.

'Keep your voice down!'

'Did Mandeep escape?'

'What does it look like?' John said, sounding cross.

Mandeep was in the room. He bent down and

tugged at the rug, positioning it to hide the crack of light beneath the door.

'What are you doing?' she said. 'Why aren't you escaping?'

'He says he doesn't want to.' John sat down heavily on his bed. 'I got him out but now he won't leave.'

'It is true,' Mandeep said. 'I won't.'

John shook his head in despair. 'But I got you out!' he repeated.

Elsie felt sorry for him. No matter how hard John tried to do something amazing, it never worked.

'Why won't you go?' she asked Mandeep.

'Because of certain things that Mr Agarwal told me.'

'Mr Agarwal?'

Mandeep crossed the room and sat on the floor with his back against the wall.

'The *khansama*,' he explained. 'The cook. He brought me a plate of food. He has an unfriendly look, but he is not unfriendly at all. He told me he is new here, he only arrived two days ago. Also, that there are three more guests due to arrive tomorrow.

With Mr Gordon and Sowerby, that will make five for the hunt.'

'We already know that!' John said.

Mandeep nodded. 'Yes. But then Mr Agarwal said that all the guests will shoot a tiger each. He was told it always happens that way.'

'Look, I know that's awful,' John interrupted. 'I know how much you hate hunting, but there's nothing you can do to stop it, Mandeep. And you're in big trouble. That beast Gordon has got it in for you.' He glanced at Elsie. 'Sowerby made that pretty clear, didn't he?'

She nodded. 'He wants to turn you over to the authorities.'

'*Now* do you see?' John said.

Mandeep wasn't listening. He stared at a point on the wall, frowning.

'There is something all wrong about this place,' he said in a quiet voice.

Elsie leaned forward. So Mandeep felt it too. Even before she'd seen the contents of Sowerby's room, from the instant she'd stepped into the building, and even earlier, in the black-green tunnel that led to the lodge, she had sensed it.

Something all wrong.

'But what is it?' she said.

Mandeep turned his eyes to John. 'There is a photograph in your father's club. It is on the wall of the lobby, not far from the entrance. I saw it once when—' He broke off. 'It is a picture of hunters and the tigers they have killed. Have you seen it?'

'I don't know,' John said. 'I don't remember. What has it got to do with anything?'

'The tigers are piled one on top of the other like sacks of grain,' Mandeep said in a wondering voice. 'One on top of the other, so many I could not count them.'

'What about it?' John said. 'It's just an old picture.'

'Exactly. It is old. Sixty or seventy years ago, maybe more. In a time when there were a lot of tigers. But now…' Mandeep shrugged.

'Now there aren't many left,' Elsie said, suddenly understanding. 'They've been hunted too much.'

It was something she'd learned on that trip to the wildlife centre. How people used to think that no matter how many animals they killed, there would always be plenty more.

'I think I know what you're getting at,' John said. 'You mean...'

'Yes,' Mandeep said. 'In the forests around here, a good *shikari* with a team of beaters might find one tiger – two, if he was lucky. But even with all the luck in the world, he would not find *four.*'

'It does seem rather odd, now you mention it,' John said.

'How is it possible?' Elsie said.

'I don't know,' Mandeep admitted.

'So *that's* why you won't leave,' John said.

'I want to find out what is going on,' Mandeep said.

John opened his mouth as if he was about to keep arguing. Then he shut it.

'All right,' he said at last. 'I didn't listen to you before and look where that got us. So, if you need help, I'm in.'

'I'm in too,' Elsie said, although the others didn't seem to hear her. They were already busy plotting.

'Best if you go back to the outhouse.'

'Yes, we don't want them looking for me.'

'I'll have to bolt the door, how will you—'

'There is a small window, if you left it unlatched, I could get out that way.'

'No point trying to look around while it's still dark.'

'No. Better to wait until dawn...'

'We can look too,' Elsie said when she could get a word in edgeways.

John nodded. 'She's right. Between the three of us, we're bound to find *something*.'

They looked at each other silently, and then Mandeep stood up. Elsie didn't want him to go back to the bleak, lonely outhouse, but she knew it made sense. She lay down on her bed, her legs curled tight with excitement, the geckos on the ceiling completely forgotten.

Thirty-five

*H*e had made the kill just before sunrise. A fully grown barasingha deer, its antlers branching to a dozen tips. The tiger had stalked the animal for some time, his belly low, his head stretched out, moving like a snake does; without seeming to move at all, but for the slightest quivering of his hips. He paused at the edge of the pool where the barasingha stood knee-deep, a little apart from the herd.

The bond between the tiger and his prey ran deep. He knew the barasingha nearly as well as he knew himself. The tilt of its narrow face, the white, watchful roll of its eye, the tug of its jaws as it grazed among the reeds. The tiger stared at it and knew even its thoughts.

For a single, unblinking, deadly instant, he *became* it.

His tail swayed, searching for perfect balance. Then he exploded into the water, covering the distance in two enormous bounds, feeling the rush of certainty that always came with action; the joy that every living thing experiences when it is doing what it was made to do.

The barasingha was hardly aware of the tiger's presence before he was on top of it, his forepaw digging into its shoulder, the other whipping around in an embrace from which there could be no escape. The tiger searched for its windpipe with his long, canine teeth. His jaw tightened.

He held on, feeling each jerk and twitch of the struggling deer's limbs, waiting with a steady, almost tender patience for the breath to leave its body, the forest growing light around him. Then he rose and shook himself and began the work of dragging his kill to cover.

He had eaten, rested, and eaten again before finally setting off in the late afternoon, heading towards the ridge of low mountains where his ruined palace lay. He made his way with the same caution as before, although he encountered nothing more alarming than a pair of furrowed tracks crossing one of the wider trails. The tiger sniffed and caught the faint, unpleasant tang of oil and rubber.

Later, he came across a clearing in the hills. There were buildings, the signs of humans all around. The tiger drew back, making a detour to avoid the area. He had covered almost a mile when he arrived at a second, smaller clearing and another building, which was completely dark. He heard sounds and stopped.

The sounds came again; calls repeated in voices both familiar and terrifyingly strange. The tiger whined and padded back and forth along the length of the building, his head down, his nostrils flooded with the rank, desperate odour coming from behind the wall.

He was used to danger. Danger was something that demanded a reaction. One faced it or fled from it, depending on the situation. But this threat felt different. There was nothing about it that the tiger understood. Only that it seemed to come not just from the outside, but from deep within him too; an anguished fascination that kept him there in the dusty clearing, when every other instinct was urging him to leave.

Holding his body close to the ground, the hairs rising on the back of his neck, he crept into a nearby thicket and lay still.

Waiting.

Thirty-six

The plan had seemed simple in the middle of the night. But in the clear light of day, Elsie and John soon realised it was going to be more complicated than they'd thought.

They were woken by a young boy carrying their washed and folded clothes, and two cups of tea which he placed silently by their beds before vanishing. They dressed, and after a solitary breakfast in the kitchen, John gathered up his courage and went to find Sowerby. He was still holding on to the hope that a jeep might be sent to fetch his father.

'Worth a shot, at least,' he said.

'Good luck,' Elsie said, feeling anxious for him.

He was gone for nearly an hour, and when he returned, his face was grim. Elsie was back in the bedroom, staring rather hopelessly out of the window.

'It's no good,' John announced, shutting the door and flinging himself down on his bed. 'He made me wait for ages and ages, and then he said it was out of the question. He couldn't spare a man to drive the jeep, not with three more guests due to arrive this morning. I knew he'd make up some excuse, I *knew* it.'

He paused, thinking. 'And that's not all. He says we're not to go outside, and gave me a lot of nonsense about a rabid dog that the servants haven't managed to catch and put down yet. It's roaming around the area, apparently.'

'A rabid dog?'

'I haven't seen or heard a single dog since we got here! Have you?'

She shook her head.

'It's just another excuse,' John said.

'I tried going out while you were talking to Sowerby,' Elsie said. 'I wanted to look around, like we said, but I didn't get very far.'

She'd found a door in the kitchen that led to

the outside and had opened it tentatively, her heart thumping. It was cool, the sky still pearly, a light breeze carrying the smell of wood smoke and kerosene. Beyond the enclosure with its scattering of trees, she saw a track that ran for a short distance before winding into the forest.

Elsie headed for the track, walking casually.

I'm just out for a stroll, she told herself.

She stopped by a tree and looked up, as though studying its branches. The tree was under siege, wrapped in the grip of an invading banyan plant. The sinister tendrils had already crept halfway up the trunk, pushing the tree's roots aside and sending clutching fingers over a nearby boulder. As if they were trying to strangle the rock itself, Elsie thought with a dart of unease.

There was a slight sound. She turned.

The man in the turban who had shown them to Sowerby's room was standing a short distance away, looking straight at her. Elsie didn't know where he'd come from.

'Hello,' she said, giving him an uncertain smile.

He didn't answer. Perhaps he hadn't heard.

'I'm just out for a stroll,' she said in a slightly louder voice.

Still he said nothing. Elsie walked on a few more paces. She paused, scuffing the ground with her foot, then looked back again. He was still there.

He was watching her, she thought. And if she tried to go any further, she felt sure he would follow.

'Well, I suppose I should be getting back,' she said, trying to make her voice sound breezy.

He gave a brief nod and gestured for her to come. Elsie trailed after him around the building to the verandah. He held the front door open and waited while she went through.

'Thanks,' Elsie muttered, feeling stupid.

It was obvious that Sowerby had no intention of letting either her or John explore the place by themselves.

'Do you think Mandeep has found anything?' Elsie asked.

'He'd have told us if he had,' John said.

'But how can he tell us if we're being watched all the time?'

She heard a clattering on the metal roof of the

kitchen. The monkeys were back. There were even more than before.

'Mr Agarwal is feeding them,' Elsie said.

The cook was standing by the kitchen door, a large bowl of scraps under his arm. Monkeys clustered around his feet, tugging at his trouser legs with eager paws. One had actually clambered up to his shoulder and was sitting with its tail draped around Mr Agarwal's neck, tearing an orange to pieces with its teeth.

'I hope nobody's left a window open,' John said. 'Monkeys can destroy a room in minutes.'

But the cook didn't seem worried. He distributed the scraps carefully, doing his best to give each animal a share, his bad-tempered face softened by pleasure. He liked being appreciated, Elsie thought. Perhaps the monkeys were the only ones who actually enjoyed his strange-tasting food.

Thirty-seven

*I*f Elsie and John couldn't go outside to look around, they decided they would at least find out all they could from Sowerby's guests.

The guests arrived mid-morning. Elsie and John were sitting in a corner of the common room, playing draughts to pass the time, although John took so long to make each move that Elsie was starting to wish she'd never suggested the game.

'It's your turn,' she reminded him for the tenth time.

'I'm *thinking*.' He placed the tip of his finger on one of his pieces, frowned, and took it off again.

Mr Gordon sat reading on the other side of the room, a glass of whisky by his side. He made a slurping noise as he sipped, sucking on his damp moustache.

The sound of approaching vehicles broke the silence. Mr Gordon sat up straight, swallowing the rest of his drink in a gulp.

'Looks like the others have got here,' he said. 'Time to make yourselves scarce. We don't want children hanging around.'

Elsie and John didn't move. He didn't have the right to tell them what to do.

There were voices in the hallway, and then the bearer opened the door to the common room and the newcomers trooped in, a woman and two men, with Sowerby bringing up the rear.

They milled around for a moment or two, shaking hands and exchanging how-do-you-dos. One of the men was older, of average height and build, apart from an enormous, jutting stomach, straining at the seams of a safari suit so new it still had all its creases.

'The name's Nottle,' he said in an American accent. 'W. Nottle.'

'May I ask what the "W" stands for?' It was the woman who had spoken. She was wearing a sailor cap perched at a stylish angle and red, sticky-looking lipstick.

'Wylie, often shortened to "Wy",' the American said. 'Geddit?'

The others looked blank.

'Play on words,' Nottle said. 'Wy Nottle. *Why Not-tle*. Always been a motto of mine, you know.'

'How very… clever,' the woman said after a second or two of silence. 'I'm Marjorie, and this is my…' She paused, her voice fluttering. 'My *husband*, Charles.'

They found seats around the fireplace, still busy with their introductions. No one seemed to notice Elsie and John sitting quietly in the corner.

'I take it you're all keen hunters,' Gordon was saying. 'I can't wait to get out there myself.'

'I'm here mainly for research, as a matter of fact,' Nottle announced, reaching with some difficulty across his stomach to take a sandwich from the bearer's tray. 'Own a theme park, largest on the West Coast. HappyHappy Land. Maybe you've heard of it.'

'Well, we have now. Ha! Ha! Ha!' Charles said.

'Twice the happiness of any other theme park,'

Nottle said, winking at Marjorie. 'Geddit?'

Gordon made a coughing sound. 'Research?'

'I'm planning a new addition to the park. Safari ride type of thing. Jeeps on a track going through trees and bushes. Same idea as a rifle range, only visitors wear pith helmets and take pot shots at tigers. Get three hits and your next ride is free!'

'Won't you need rather a lot of tigers?' Charles ventured. 'Frightfully hard to find a steady supply, you know.'

Nottle's stomach shifted up and down as he chuckled. 'We won't be using actual animals! Ever heard of animatronics? My tigers are going to be the biggest and the best. *Far* more impressive than the real thing...'

'Well, we're here on our honeymoon,' Marjorie said abruptly, as if she'd decided it was time for her to be the centre of attention. She smiled babyishly at Charles. 'It's all still so *new*,' she said in a breathy voice. 'Isn't it, darling?'

'Got hitched only last week,' Charles agreed. 'Ha! Ha! Ha!'

Elsie wondered why he was laughing. Did he find everything funny? But there was another, far more disturbing question.

How was killing animals anyone's idea of a *honeymoon*?

She glanced over at Sowerby sitting a little apart. He took a drag on his cigarette, his eyes flickering to the clock on the far wall. He was bored by the lot of them, Elsie decided. He was only there because he had to be polite…

Her thoughts were interrupted by a cry of delight. 'Children!'

Marjorie had finally spotted them. She clasped her hands together rapturously. 'You didn't tell me there'd be children!'

'Don't know why they're still here,' Gordon muttered. 'Ought to have gone home by now.'

'I *love* children,' Marjorie said, 'don't I, Charles? Come over here, let's see you, then! Oh, one of them is a little *girl*!'

She gestured to Elsie, 'Come *on*, don't be shy!'

'Marjorie won't bite, will you, Marjorie? Ha! Ha! Ha!'

Elsie advanced awkwardly.

'What's your name, sweetie?' Marjorie said, as if she were talking to a three-year-old.

Up close, she had a clownish look, her lipstick bleeding into the fine lines around her mouth.

'Are you here to go hunting?' she said. 'With your own ickle, lickle gun? How old are you, pet?'

Nobody spoke like that to Kelsie Corvette, Elsie thought, with a flash of outrage. They wouldn't dare. She lifted her chin and gave Marjorie a level stare.

'Eleven,' she said. 'And a *half*.'

Nottle gave a snort of laughter. 'She sure got you there!'

Marjorie flushed. She stared at Elsie with narrowed eyes.

'Aren't you a little old to be playing dress-up?' she said, fastening her gaze on Elsie's trainers. 'Where on earth did you get those peculiar things?'

It was a spiteful question. But it was also a lucky one, because it made Elsie hang her head with embarrassment. And if she hadn't been staring down at precisely that moment, she wouldn't have noticed something lying on the floor nearby. If anyone else had seen it, they might have thought a gust of wind had blown it through the crack beneath the door. But Elsie knew that it had been deliberately pushed.

It was a small yellow feather.

Thirty-eight

Mandeep had sent them a message. He must have found something. Elsie glanced at John, but he was still in the corner, doing his best to blend with the wallpaper.

'Well, where did you get them from?' Marjorie repeated. Everyone was now staring at Elsie's trainers.

'Real strange,' Nottle said. 'Take 'em off. 'Let's have a look at 'em.'

Elsie felt a stab of panic. She shook her head.

'Do as you're told,' Marjorie snapped.

'I *can't*…'

'Why ever not?'

'Because,' Elsie said frantically. 'Because… I think I'm going to be sick.'

'*Oh!*' Marjorie cried, jerking back. 'Not here, get away from me, get away!'

'Was it something you ate?' Charles suggested. 'My sandwich tasted a bit rum, now I come to think of it.'

'I just need some fresh air...'

'Go at once, this *minute*.' Marjorie fanned herself in an exaggerated fashion. 'You don't think it could be catching, do you, Charles? On our *honeymoon*...'

Elsie darted gratefully for the door. She paused to make sure nobody was following her, then hurried across the deserted lobby and on to the verandah.

'Mandeep?'

She walked along the verandah to the far end and looked over the edge. He was standing below, hidden in the shadow of the wall.

'I saw your feather,' Elsie whispered.

'Where is John?'

'He's inside, it's hard to get out without somebody seeing. Did you find anything?'

Mandeep nodded, his eyes wide.

'What is it?'

'I must show you. Can you come?'

Elsie hesitated. But there was nobody around. They were all busy attending to the guests. She followed Mandeep around the back of the building and on to the track on the far side of the clearing.

'Where are we going?'

Mandeep didn't reply. He quickened his pace, not slowing even after the track curved away and the lodge was hidden from sight. Elsie stared into the tangled darkness on either side.

'It's far,' Mandeep said. 'A mile, maybe more.'

Elsie wanted to ask him again where they were going, but his face wore a look of such fierce urgency that she felt almost frightened. He walked with jerky speed, his arms tense. She had to half-run to keep up with him.

After about fifteen minutes, he turned on to a smaller path, and then another, even smaller and more overgrown. They followed it for a while until it petered out.

'It's a dead end,' Elsie said.

'That is what I thought too. But then I heard something…' Mandeep bent and parted the screen of bushes. Elsie saw the wisp of a trail leading through low clumps of bamboo. It was blocked by the knotted trunk of a strangler vine, the wood twisted like a snake paralysed in mid-throttle.

'It has been put there to stop people getting through,' Mandeep said.

They scrambled over with difficulty, and even Elsie had to crouch as they followed the trail, pushing through undergrowth as they went. After what seemed ages, it grew lighter ahead, and they emerged into a clearing worn smooth by tyre tracks.

A long, low, windowless building, roofed with corrugated iron, stood in the centre, and from it came a sound.

It wasn't loud, but it was somehow vast. A rasp of breath and then a yawning groan, so strange in its utter, terrifying wildness that Elsie's mind seemed to freeze for a second. It came again, unearthly, desolate.

'What's *that*?'

Mandeep looked at her with misery in his eyes.

'Tiger,' he said.

There was a door at the far end of the building.

Mandeep lifted the wooden bar and tugged it open. Elsie peered inside, her legs trembling, her breath catching on a sharp, fetid smell.

The interior was almost completely dark, apart from a few rays of light slanting through rusted holes in the roof. She blinked, trying to adjust her eyes, saw the light catch a sliver of gold, as if its touch had burned the darkness. The shape of bars emerged, a groove in the concrete floor running darkly wet between.

She heard a growl, the sound deep in her bones.

Cages. Lining both sides of the room.

Elsie gasped and took a step back. But Mandeep's hand was on her arm, nudging her forward. The foul, musky smell was far stronger inside, although she scarcely noticed. Her attention was fixed on the shadowy forms behind the bars. She could *feel* them. In the prickle of her skin and the thinness of her breath and the far-off hammer of her heart.

Tigers. Four of them.

'I... don't understand.'

All the urgency had left Mandeep's face. He looked smaller suddenly, as helpless as a child, his hand clutching the front of his jacket, his eyes glistening in the dim light.

It hurts him to see this, Elsie thought. *It hurts so much it makes him cry.*

'What's going on?' she whispered.

'They are for Sowerby's hunt,' Mandeep said. 'I am sure of it.'

Elsie nodded. It was the only explanation that made sense.

Mr Gordon had told them that Sowerby was a legendary hunter. But even Sowerby couldn't find animals if they weren't actually there. The only way he could provide a tiger for each one of his guests was if he caught the tigers first. He must have ranged far and wide to trap them. That was why he didn't hold hunts very often. He needed time to find the animals.

Time to find the guests as well. People rich enough to afford the huge cost. People like Mr

Gordon who were no good at hunting themselves, and too ignorant to know when they were being duped.

Sowerby must be making a fortune.

Elsie became aware of how hot it was in the building, how airless. A stink rose from the central gutter, filled with the run-off from the hosed-down floor and the dank cages.

Mandeep began to walk along the centre of the room, gazing through the bars at each of the tigers in turn. Elsie followed hesitantly, keeping a safe distance from the cages. But the animals hardly seemed to notice them. Two were lying on their sides, motionless except for an occasional twitch of their tails. Another stood, panting, with lowered head and lips pulled back in a strangely fixed grimace. The fourth paced mindlessly back and forth, turning every few steps when it reached the side of its cage. It paused for a second, a shudder rippling its tawny hide, then swung its head and began to pace again.

'Why… are they like that?' she asked Mandeep. 'What's wrong with them?'

'I think that they have been drugged.'

'Are you sure?'

'It is probably how they were caught. And now they are being kept drugged to make them quiet and easier to handle.'

'And easier to shoot,' Elsie pointed out. Sowerby would release them tomorrow, she thought. They would be too doped to get far. Perfect targets for even the lamest of hunters.

She turned to Mandeep with a sudden idea. 'Listen, the guests seem really horrible. Two of them are on their *honeymoon*.' Elsie's face twisted in disgust. 'But I don't think even *they* would like it if they knew the hunt was rigged. I mean, they want to kill tigers, but not like this. They don't want to feel like fools.'

Mandeep didn't say anything. He was too busy examining the door of one of the cages, frowning in concentration.

'If they knew what was going on, I bet they'd be really angry with Sowerby,' Elsie continued eagerly. 'I wouldn't be surprised if they asked for their money back and made him cancel the whole thing. We have to go back and tell them.'

Mandeep looked at her. He shook his head.

'No. What we have to do is free these tigers.'

The instant he said it, Elsie knew he was right. The guests might get angry, cancel the hunt, go home in outrage, but it would only be because they felt cheated. Not because they cared what happened to the tigers. And the tigers were all that mattered.

She nodded and saw relief leap in Mandeep's eyes.

'But we can't just… let them go,' she said, giving the animals a nervous glance. 'I mean, what if they…?'

Mandeep turned back to the cage. 'I do not know how the doors open. You are right, it would need to be at a safe distance.'

'They look like electric locks,' Elsie said, staring at the metal boxes attached to each cage. 'You see here? I bet this little button lights up when the lock is activated.' She trotted back to the entrance, searching the wall on either side of the door.

'There aren't any switches here, but they must be somewhere. Maybe back at the lodge.'

She reached up and removed a couple of objects from a shelf by the door, then turned to show them to Mandeep. 'These might come in useful,' she said, feeling pleased with herself. 'I didn't know walkie-talkies had been invented yet!'

Thirty-nine

They were quiet on the way back. Mandeep didn't want to return to the outhouse. He would rather hide somewhere nearby instead.

'What if they come looking for you?' Elsie asked.

'It is worth the risk. It will be hard to find me if I stay in one place.'

They were about half a mile from the lodge when Elsie saw a turning off the main track, ending in a short flight of stone stairs.

'What's up there?'

The stairs were wet and uneven with age. She had to pick her way carefully until she reached the top. Then she stopped still in astonishment.

She was standing at the edge of a glade, fringed by trees. At the far end, above a pool of dark green water, a vast statue lay stretched out. He lay as though asleep, one knee raised, his head resting on a pillow of stone, his calm face tilted to the side. Time had weathered him, blurring his outline under the downy creep of moss and yellow lichen. In places he was quite worn away. Yet this only seemed to deepen the stillness and serenity of his ancient features.

As if he had lain so long there dreaming, he had become the dream itself.

Mandeep pressed the palms of his hands together and briefly bowed his head.

'Lord Vishnu,' he said. 'The god of well-being and protection.'

A hush filled the glade. All Elsie could hear was the murmur of insects and the sound of water trickling down stone to break the surface of the pool.

'This place must be very old,' she whispered.

'Hundreds of years,' Mandeep agreed.

They went to the edge of the pool and gazed for a while in silence at the shrine. Then they turned to take in the view. The shrine had been built on the edge of the hillside, below the land stretched away towards a flat-topped mountain, far in the distance.

It was breezy up there, the wind filled with the scent of basil and honey and warm, dry grass. Elsie could see the whole forest spread beneath her. Down on the ground, it had seemed a confusing place, full of unseen obstacles and odd changes of terrain. It was different from above. She could see how everything fitted together. The groves of trees and tangled thickets, the sunlit meadows, the shining threads of streams. As if it had been planned to the last detail.

'It's all laid out,' she said in a wondering voice.

'Like a garden,' Mandeep said. 'So, you see it too.'

'Yes,' she said, smiling at him.

The sun was no longer directly overhead. It was early afternoon already. Elsie was suddenly aware of how long she had been gone from the lodge. It must be well over an hour.

'I have to get back,' she said in alarm. 'What if they're looking for me?'

There was a cave in the rocky slope behind the statue of Lord Vishnu, although it was so cramped that Mandeep had to crawl on hands and knees to enter it. But it made a fine hiding place.

'Are you sure you'll be all right?'

'It is better than the outhouse,' Mandeep said from the darkness.

Elsie handed him his bag, hesitated for an anxious second and then hurried back down the stone steps to the track below.

Forty

Mr Gordon was on the verandah as she approached the lodge. It was no use ducking away, he had already seen her. He was resting his elbows against the railing, a bored look on his face.

'What've *you* been up to?' he said, without straightening up.

Elsie had prepared a story to explain her absence, although she knew that as stories go, it wasn't a terribly good one.

'I went out because I felt sick and then a monkey stole my scarf,' she said in a rush. 'I chased it, but it got away. Into the bushes,' she added.

'You weren't wearing a scarf,' he said in an indifferent manner, as if he wasn't particularly curious, and merely wanted to catch her out in a lie.

'It was in my pocket,' Elsie said. 'Sort of hanging out a bit…' Her voice trailed off.

He stared at her.

'It was a red scarf,' Elsie said. 'I think that's why the monkey wanted it because of, you know, the red colour.'

She waited for him to say he didn't believe a word of it. But he only shrugged, apparently losing interest.

Elsie hesitated. If she and Mandeep were right, and Sowerby intended to release the caged tigers from a safe distance, he must be planning on letting them go one by one. He would hardly want his guests coming across them all at once. But she still didn't understand how Sowerby knew which direction each tiger would take.

'How will you find the tigers tomorrow?' she asked Mr Gordon. 'Are they difficult to hunt?'

His face lit up at the question. 'Sowerby knows their movements like the back of his hand. I've heard he can lead you right up to them.'

'So, you'll just walk until you find one?'

'It's a little more complicated than that,' Mr

Gordon said with a patronising chuckle. 'We'll go in the jeeps to start with, find a likely spot. Then set out on foot with the guns. There'll be four or five beaters going ahead of us, making a racket with their sticks to flush out the animals.'

'Why don't the beaters have guns too?' Elsie asked. 'What if a tiger attacks them?'

'Oh, you don't need to worry about that,' Mr. Gordon said, with another chuckle. 'You'd be amazed how quickly those chaps can climb a tree.'

Elsie stared at him. He was the most horrible human being she had ever met in her life, she thought. After Sowerby.

She turned without another word and went into the lodge.

John was no longer in the common room, although everyone else was still there. Sowerby glanced up sharply as she opened the door.

'Feeling better?'

Elsie nodded. 'I felt ill for ages and ages,' she stammered. 'I sat outside.'

'Close to the lodge,' she added. 'Just *sitting*.'

But Sowerby was too distracted to pay much

attention. Nottle was looming close through the fog of cigarette smoke.

'I'm thinking of calling my new addition to the park, "Tiger Terror-tory",' he was saying. 'Neat name, don't you think? Play on words, you know…'

Elsie closed the door silently and hurried down the corridor to the bedroom, looking for John.

Forty-one

It was difficult for Elsie to tell John about everything that had happened because he wouldn't keep still. He kept pacing rather like the caged tigers had done, although a hundred times less gracefully, his hands rammed into the pockets of his wrinkled shorts. Every few seconds he interrupted Elsie with an exclamation.

'Rotter! Utter bounder! How many cages did you say? Are they marked?'

'I'm trying to tell you,' Elsie said. 'I can't think straight with you striding around like that.'

There were six cages, each with a number painted on the door, and the four tigers were adult animals, apart from a small female who Mandeep said was not fully grown, probably less than a year old.

'Mandeep could tell straight away they'd been drugged,' Elsie told John. 'They weren't acting like they normally do.'

John stopped moving. He looked at Elsie.

'I say, are you thinking what I'm thinking?'

'How do I know what you're thinking?'

'The *tiger*,' John said. 'The one I nearly shot. It wasn't acting normally either.'

Elsie thought of the animal she had seen in the clearing. Its body motionless, its neck held low, as if sinking beneath the weight of its own head.

'Do you think it was drugged too?'

'Maybe...' John paused, nodding to himself. 'Yes. Sowerby could have shot it with the drug and then it escaped before he could trap it. Must have happened recently because the drug hadn't worn off yet.'

He lifted his head. 'I'd have got it if you hadn't stopped me, couldn't have missed at that range. I'd convinced myself it was a man-eater. Gave you rather a hard time about it. Like to say sorry for that. Person ought to admit when he's wrong,' he added, holding out his hand solemnly.

'It's okay,' Elsie muttered, shaking his hand.

They sat down on their beds a little awkwardly, facing each other.

'So now what?' John said. 'We need to make a plan.'

Elsie liked how he said 'we'.

'There must be a way to open those cages,' she said. 'I thought the locks were electric, but I didn't see any wiring. There wasn't even a light switch.'

John was silent for a moment, thinking.

'Radio waves!' he exclaimed.

'What about them?'

'My father told me, during the war, they had a device that used radio waves to guide missiles and tanks at the enemy from a safe distance. Maybe Sowerby's got something similar to open the locks.'

'Like a remote for the door of the garage…'

'A *what*?'

'Never mind,' Elsie said.

'Did you see any kind of antenna?'

'Yes, I did, come to think of it,' Elsie said. It had looked like an old-fashioned TV aerial, sticking up from the roof of the building.

'That's it, then! We've got to search for some kind of device that uses radio waves. Probably looks a bit like a radio itself.'

Elsie pulled the walkie-talkie from the waistband of her jeans.

'Mandeep has the other one. It's so we can tell him when we find out how to get the cages unlocked. Only I'm not sure it's working...'

'You're doing it wrong,' John said, trying to grab the walkie-talkie. 'Have you even switched it on?'

'Yes, I have!' Elsie said, fiddling with the buttons.

'You're not supposed to turn that dial.'

'Why? What does it do?'

'How should I know?' John said. 'You're meant to press *there* when you want to talk. On the side...'

'I knew that,' Elsie said, holding down the button. 'Hello?' she whispered. 'Are you there?'

'You're meant to say, "hello, *over*,"' John said, finally managing to get hold of the walkie-talkie. 'Hello, *over*. Come in, Mandeep, *over*.'

He didn't need to be so self-important, Elsie thought. She was the one who'd found the walkie-talkies, after all.

'This is John speaking, *over.*'

The walkie-talkie crackled, and she heard Mandeep, his voice sounding as if it came from a great way off.

'Can you hear… am in… to unlock them?'

'Keep the button pushed *down* when you're talking,' John said. '*Over.*'

'Over what?' Mandeep said.

'Forget it,' John said, heaving a sigh of exasperation. 'Look, stay where you are in the cave. We'll let you know when we find anything.'

'You must hurry,' Mandeep said. There was a burst of static. 'Good luck.'

'Good luck to you too,' John said. 'Over and out.'

'I hope it wasn't a mistake for him to leave the outhouse,' John told Elsie.

'They'll just think he went home, won't they?'

'Probably. But if Sowerby suspects anything, he's bound to put a guard on that building,' John said. 'I reckon he'd have done it already if he had more people working for him. He must be paying the staff a lot to keep their mouths shut and do his dirty work.'

'Do you think Mr Agarwal knows about the tigers?' Elsie wondered.

'Must do.'

Elsie thought of the cook's face as he'd fed the monkeys that morning. Maybe he did know what was going on. But she couldn't believe he felt happy about it.

Forty-two

Although Elsie had told John about the building in the clearing, and the tigers, and how Mandeep had found a place to hide, there was something she'd left out of her account. It was too difficult to explain, and since John didn't believe she was from the future, there wasn't much point trying.

It had happened when she and Mandeep were on their way back, before they'd discovered the shrine.

'Mandeep,' Elsie had said quickly, before she could change her mind, 'do you know about a plant called "the flower that catches time"?'

She'd been wanting to ask him this question ever since she'd met him, although it had never felt like the right moment. It still didn't, but Elsie wasn't sure if she'd get another chance.

Mandeep glanced at her in surprise. 'Where did you hear of it?'

'I… read about it. In a book.'

He was silent, and Elsie plunged on. 'It said in the book that it has some sort of… I don't know, some sort of power. Or people believe that, anyway.'

'My grandfather thought so,' Mandeep said. 'But he was old and very sick.'

'What did he say about it?'

'He was lost, a long way from home when he saw the flower. Five years ago, he said.' Mandeep's voice was soft with sadness. 'Then he said it had been when he was a young man. So, you see, he was all muddled up.'

'What happened when he saw it?'

'It was the most beautiful flower he had ever seen, he told me, with a fragrance like no other. After he found it, all the broken things in our lives were mended, and our family's troubles were put right. That was when I knew his fever must be very high.'

'Why?'

Mandeep smiled. 'Our family has never had troubles. We are healthy and happy, my parents have good jobs and many friends. We are fortunate.'

Elsie caught her breath. Mandeep's grandfather had gone back in time. He must have done. He'd changed his family's past somehow and turned the luck of all their years to come. She was probably the only person in the world who knew the truth.

'Did he say anything else?' she asked, trying to keep the eagerness out of her voice. 'Like, how the flower actually worked its power, how long it lasted, that kind of thing?'

'No. But he had a seed. He gave it to me just before he died.'

So that's how you got it! Elsie almost said.

Mandeep patted the side of his body. 'It is in my secret pocket, along with other treasures.'

'You keep it in your jacket?' Elsie stumbled, suddenly uncertain of her feet.

He'd show it to her if she asked, she thought. He'd hand it over without question. She could wander a little way off and drop it, as if by accident. Somewhere in the undergrowth, where he wouldn't have a chance of finding it again. It would be easy. And then –

Then Mandeep would never give the seed to John as a parting gift when John left India. And John would never plant it, nor keep it for years until it reached its time to bloom.

It would not be waiting on that far future morning, when she'd wake at dawn to find the greenhouse door ajar. Instead, nothing but ferns and trailing jasmine, misty in the light of another, perfectly ordinary day.

All she had to do was take the seed from Mandeep and she would be back, having breakfast with Great-Uncle John. Eating bacon. Safe.

She wouldn't vanish from this place. *She would simply never have been here.*

'Are you okay?' Mandeep said, stopping and giving her a puzzled look.

But then –

Then John would shoot the tiger. And neither he or Mandeep would meet Mr Gordon, or go to the lodge, or discover what Sowerby kept in the building with the metal roof. The hunt would happen just as it always did.

'What is the matter?' Mandeep said. 'Are you feeling ill?'

Elsie closed her eyes and saw the tigers, padding out one by one, dazed in the sunlight. The hunters ready for them. Marjorie's red lips parted in anticipation, Mr Gordon's glasses aglitter, Nottle's belly heaving with excitement...

She drew a ragged breath.

'I'm fine,' she told Mandeep, trying to smile. 'Nothing's the matter.'

His face cleared. 'We must hurry.'

Elsie nodded, and they kept walking, although she found herself dragging her feet. She couldn't help thinking that she might have just lost her one chance of getting home. It was hard to look on the bright side of *that*.

Then it came to her. True, it was more of a glimmer than a bright side, yet it was enough to lift her step a little. Mandeep's grandfather had travelled to the past, like her. But he'd done more than that.

He had also managed to come back again.

Forty-three

It was one thing to decide to search the lodge, quite another to actually do it. Neither Elsie nor John had a clear idea of exactly what it was they were looking for, which meant it could be anywhere. In addition, the lodge was full of people. The guests were still in the common room. Elsie could hear voices and snatches of laughter each time the servants opened the common room door to deliver yet another tray of food and drinks.

'Won't they ever stop jawing?' John said. 'Don't they have anything better to do?'

Elsie and John sat in the bedroom, waiting. It was almost three o'clock before they heard a commotion in the hallway. The guests had finally emerged.

'Do me some good to get a little exercise,'

they heard Nottle say.

'Is it far, Mr Sowerby?' Marjorie said, her voice rising above the general hubbub. 'Poor Charles has a dicky leg...'

'Kept me out of the war, you know. Fearful shame. Ha! Ha! Ha!'

'Charles was *so* disappointed...'

Elsie and John looked at each other, hardly able to believe their luck. From the sound of it, all the guests had decided to leave the lodge at once.

'Come on,' John said. 'This is our chance.'

They found them milling around in the lobby, Marjorie reapplying her lipstick, Charles trying out walking sticks from a selection by the front door.

'Where are you going?' Elsie asked. Marjorie glanced at her, then looked away.

'We're off to see an old relic,' Nottle said.

'Relic?' Elsie said, her voice faltering with sudden premonition.

'A shrine to the god Vishnu,' Nottle said. 'Not far from here apparently, the bearer is going to show us the way.'

Elsie looked urgently at John. They had to warn

Mandeep. But the walkie-talkie was back in their room.

'*Stay here*,' John mouthed.

Elsie nodded. He edged towards the door, doing his best to look casual, then disappeared.

'I ought to change my hat,' Marjorie was fussing. 'Charles dear, can you get me the other one from our room?'

'Your topee?'

'No, that's for *tomorrow*. The khaki one, with the large brim…'

'Righty ho.'

Elsie shifted from foot to foot as they waited. Three or four minutes ticked by. If John had managed to get through to Mandeep, she thought, surely he would have been back to tell her by now. He must be still trying.

'Do hurry up, Charles,' Marjorie called.

What if there was too much static? Or Mandeep wasn't near his walkie-talkie? Charles was already returning with Marjorie's hat. In less than a minute, the guests would be on their way, and then it might be too late.

'I want to go and see the shrine!' she blurted in panic. 'Can I come too?'

Nottle shrugged amiably. 'Don't see why not.'

Perhaps she could get ahead of them, Elsie thought. If she left right now and ran all the way, she'd have plenty of time to reach Mandeep. But the bearer was standing by the door, a watchful look on his face.

Elsie had no choice. She had to stay with the group.

They set off at last, moving at a leisurely pace, although Elsie was almost hopping from dread and indecision. The bearer was walking ahead, leading them down the track. Would it look suspicious if she tried to overtake him? Would he guess she had been to the shrine before?

'Whatever is the matter?' Marjorie said. 'I do hope you're not about to be sick again.'

'Ants in her pants,' Charles said. 'That happened to me a couple of years ago, you know. Sat down for a breather, next thing I knew the blighters were all over me.'

Behind them, Gordon lashed idly at the bushes with his cane.

'Right there is the reason you ought to stick to theme parks,' Nottle told Charles. 'There aren't any ants in HappyHappy Land, not a single one.'

They were almost at the turning to the shrine. Elsie felt sweat breaking out all over her. John had probably managed to get through on the walkie-talkie by now, but she couldn't be sure. Mandeep might still have no idea they were there, he could be sitting out in plain view…

'I wonder what the shrine looks like,' she babbled. 'I can't wait to see it!'

'You don't need to shout,' Marjorie said. 'I'm not deaf.'

'I bet it's nice,' Elsie said, even louder. 'I'm really, really excited.'

The bearer had reached the turning. He stopped, gesturing them forward.

'I think we've arrived!' Elsie shrieked, darting ahead of the others. 'Oh, look at these steps!'

'Have you gone quite mad?' Marjorie's voice was tight with irritation.

'BE CAREFUL,' Elsie bellowed. 'THEY'RE A BIT SLIPPERY!'

She reached the top and cast a frantic eye around the glade. It was empty.

Mandeep had got to the cave in time.

Elsie sat down by the edge of the pool, overcome by relief.

'So, this is the famous shrine,' Gordon said.

The guests stood for a moment or two, taking in the peaceful scene.

'I thought there'd be more to it than that,' Marjorie said finally. 'There's only that old statue.'

'Rather a poor show,' Charles agreed.

Only Nottle seemed impressed. 'Kind of awe-inspiring,' he said, peering closely at the stone figure. 'Although it needs a good repair job. Can't understand why there isn't a fence around this thing. That way you could charge admission...' He straightened up. 'I tell you what, I'm going to have it in my park! A fibreglass replica, only new-looking, with all its fingers and toes.

'We'll have the pool too,' he continued in growing excitement. 'Visitors can throw coins into it... Lord Wishnoo! That's what we'll call him. *Wish*-noo, geddit?'

'Jolly good,' Charles said. 'Ha! Ha! Ha!'

Elsie looked away. It didn't matter how stupid they were. The longer they stayed talking, the longer John would have to look around the lodge.

'Hello! I've just spotted something.' It was Gordon's voice. Elsie turned to see what he was pointing at. 'See that cave?'

'What about it?' Nottle said.

'It's just the sort of place a bear might hide her cubs,' Gordon said. 'Or a tiger, come to that. I'm going to have a look.'

'Oh, do be careful,' Marjorie cried, giving him an admiring glance.

There was nothing Elsie could say or do. Gordon was making his way up the slope to the cave. He arrived and peered cautiously inside.

'Can't see a damn thing.'

Elsie clutched her hands. The cave wasn't deep, Mandeep had bumped into the far wall almost straight away.

'Use your cane!' Nottle shouted.

'Good idea.'

'Don't,' Elsie whispered. '*Don't, don't, don't.*'

It was no use, Gordon was already reaching inside. She could hear the rattle of his cane against the wall of the cave. He probed further, his face twisted with effort.

'Anything there?' Marjorie's voice was shrill.

Gordon withdrew the cane. 'Nothing,' he said with disgust. 'Clean as a whistle.'

Elsie let out her breath. Mandeep must have guessed they'd look in the cave.

He had been too clever for them.

Forty-four

John was just coming out of the lodge when they arrived back. While the guests went inside to rest in their rooms before dinner, John and Elsie found a corner of the verandah where they could talk.

'Why did you go haring off?' John demanded. 'We were meant to be searching the lodge together.'

'I wasn't sure if you'd got through to Mandeep.'

'Of course I got through! Why wouldn't I?'

'I don't know,' Elsie admitted. 'I guess I panicked.'

John shook his head in a pitying way. 'It's just like when you ran away from that pig, although it wasn't even a pig. It was more like a *piglet.*'

'It wasn't my f—'

Elsie stopped herself. They didn't have time to get into yet another argument.

'So, did you find anything?'

John shook his head. 'I looked everywhere. Well, almost everywhere.'

He had searched the common room and the lobby, and most of the downstairs, apart from the kitchen, where Mr Agarwal was busy preparing the evening meal.

'I don't think they'd keep it there, anyway,' Elsie said. 'What about the buildings outside the lodge?'

'Mostly servants' quarters, apart from Mandeep's outhouse and the generator hut.'

'What about Sowerby's room?' It was the obvious place. Elsie was surprised John hadn't looked there first.

'He was in it the whole time. Didn't come out once.'

'I bet it's there,' Elsie said. 'We didn't see it before because of all the other—'

She broke off. As if he had known they were talking about him, Sowerby suddenly appeared, a newspaper under his arm. He gave them a brief glance, then took a seat at the opposite end of the verandah. Elsie and John stared straight ahead. A bird gave a warbling cry from the depths of the trees. Sowerby shook his paper open and they heard the rustle as he turned the first page.

John looked at Elsie out of the corner of his eye. *It's your turn*, he mouthed.

Elsie shrank lower in her seat. But he was right. It was her turn.

What about the bearer? she mouthed.

John made a face. *Just be careful.*

The lobby was empty. Elsie scurried across the hall and paused at the foot of the staircase, looking around to make sure the coast was clear, her heart beating so hard it almost made her sick.

I'm Kelsie Corvette, she told herself as she crept up the stairs. *I'm Kelsie Corvette.*

The reason Kelsie Corvette wasn't afraid of anyone was because she was an expert in marshell arts, especially Juice-itsoo...

There was nobody on the landing, although the door

to one of the guest rooms was half-open and Elsie could hear Marjorie, her voice raised in complaint.

'Fearfully hot… do be a dear…'

Then the door closed, and her voice was cut off.

Elsie darted towards Sowerby's room on the far side, keeping to the wall, away from the wooden railing that lined the open area in the middle of the floor. If there was anyone in the dining room below, she didn't want them to look up and see her.

Sowerby's door was ajar. At least she didn't have to turn the handle, Elsie thought. It made entering feel like less of a crime. But not much less. As she slipped into the room, Elsie was almost light-headed with fear and guilt.

Should she close the door behind her, or leave it the way it had been? She didn't know. Her mind had gone completely blank.

She didn't have time to work it out, she had to hurry. She took a couple of steps forward, gazing around.

The room seemed even more grotesque than before. Elsie wondered how she could have mistaken the contents for ordinary knick-knacks and pieces of furniture. How skilfully the items had been constructed. Polished and gilded, inlaid with precious stones and metals, exquisite in their craftsmanship. Yet it only made them all the more hideous.

The greater their beauty, she thought, the uglier they looked.

Something chimed softly, and she froze. Yet it was only the shiver of crystal beads around the top of a lamp. They caught the sun as they moved, sending points of light dancing over the surface of the shade. It was made of something thin, almost transparent, patterned by lines like threads running through a piece of fabric.

Except it wasn't fabric. Elsie didn't know what it was, and she didn't want to know. She glanced away, her eyes ranging over the walls.

Photographs of men holding guns, a mirror framed by snakeskin with the head of the snake still attached, butterflies in rows behind glass, a vast turtle shell...

Elsie frowned, trying to concentrate. She was supposed to be searching for something that operated the locks on the cages. John had said it might look like a radio. Old-fashioned radios were huge, surely she would see it if it was here.

She crossed the room to the desk. It had claw-foot legs, only these were real claws and real feet, not carved wooden ones. There were boxes on the desk, paperweights with beetles and lizards, and slender, coiled snakes trapped in glass, a pen-holder made from the talons of an eagle, books bound in lizard skin, a gold-tipped rhino horn and three small, bright birds sitting dead on a branch under a dome. But no radio.

Then she saw it. Behind the desk, on a table by the window. A white tasselled cloth covering something bulky and square-shaped.

Even before she lifted a corner of the cloth, Elsie knew what she would find underneath. A glance confirmed it. It wasn't simply that it looked like a radio, it was also the fact that it looked so *unlike* a radio. There were too many buttons and dials and trailing wires, and it was too crude in appearance. As if it had been assembled out of bits and bobs of other things by someone not particularly worried about how it would look.

There were numbers next to the switches, although Elsie didn't wait to examine them. All she could think of was getting out of there so she could tell John. She lowered the cloth and rushed around the desk, heading for the door.

Elsie had never been good at picking up her feet, even in the best of circumstances. She was halfway across the room when her toe snagged on the curling edge of one of the animal skins that covered the floor. She pitched forward, tried to right herself, and landed with a thud at the base of the elephant tusk chair.

Her wrist hurt. It had twisted as it caught her fall. Elsie rose to her knees and rubbed it anxiously. She was about to scramble up when she heard something. It was more of a feeling than a noise. A prickling sense that she was no longer alone in the room.

'What are you doing here?' Sowerby said.

Forty-five

*H*e had entered without a sound and was standing so still that it was impossible to tell how long he had been there, his gazed fixed, an unlit cigarette motionless between the fingers of one hand.

Elsie jerked with shock.

'I was just... just... looking at this chair.'

'So I see,' Sowerby said. 'Interested in it, are you?'

'Yes,' Elsie said, seizing with desperation on the word. 'It's so *interesting*.' She stood up, her face burning. 'I saw the door was open and I know I wasn't meant to, but I thought...'

He looked at her, as though considering.

'I'm really, really sorry,' Elsie said.

Sowerby broke his stillness, tapping the end of

his cigarette against the top of his hand.

'You can sit in it, if you like,' he said.

'The chair?'

He nodded, a faint smile tugging briefly at his mouth.

'Oh... great,' Elsie said, perching awkwardly on the edge. 'Thanks.'

He believes me, she thought. *He really thinks I'm interested in his horrible things.*

In a way, he was right. Elsie couldn't deny that the room held a grim kind of fascination. Sowerby too, with his stony features and silent tread. His eyes had a flat, sunless look, as if set too deep in his head for the light to find. Perhaps that was why his face seemed so blank.

Her hands trembled. She clasped them together on her lap, partly to stop the trembling and partly so she wouldn't have to touch the smooth, ivory arms of the chair.

'It's very nice,' she whispered.

Sowerby must have taken it for a whisper of awe.

'One of my more impressive pieces,' he said.

If you were interested in something, you were

supposed to ask questions about it. Elsie racked her brains.

'Did you shoot it yourself?' she ventured at last. 'The elephant, I mean.'

'Of course. Everything in this room is a trophy of mine.'

'That must've… taken you a long time.'

'Thirty-five years.' Sowerby went to the desk and lit his cigarette, inhaling with an eager hiss. 'That was my first,' he told her, pointing to a black, spiralling horn on the mantelpiece. The horn was set on an ebony base, and the end was tipped with silver.

'A blackbuck,' Sowerby said. 'It was a difficult shot, but I got it. My father had the horn decorated to mark the occasion. After that, I did the same with all my kills.'

'But why?' Elsie asked.

He stared at her, as if surprised by her lack of understanding.

'Isn't it obvious?' Sowerby's arm swept the room. 'I had them made into treasures, don't you see? Objects of value.'

Elsie had been expecting him to give her some line about how he'd done it out of respect. As memorials to the creatures he'd shot. Something noble-sounding, about how they had been worthy opponents, and that even though he went around killing things, it was because he actually loved animals, and admired them.

That would have been bad enough, but this was far worse.

Objects of value.

As if the life of the smallest mouse wasn't worth more than everything in that room put together.

Yet Sowerby was blind to it. All he understood was having and getting. All he cared about was *owning*.

It was a dreadful thought, but for some reason it made Elsie feel a little less frightened of the man, and she got up at once from his chair. How long had she been in the room? It felt like an hour. John would be wondering what had happened to her.

She glanced at the clock. It was set in a skull, the bone white as the purest marble, two long, curved teeth framing the clock face, as if devouring time itself.

'Tiger,' Sowerby said. 'The largest I ever saw.'

'Mr Gordon said you're a tiger expert,' Elsie commented. 'He said he didn't know how you manage to get so many.'

I know how you manage it, she thought.

'Tigers have been a lifelong interest of mine,' Sowerby said. 'I've studied them for years, using the very latest technology.'

Elsie didn't say anything. She remembered the caged tigers, their fire almost extinguished in the stinking darkness. He was nothing but a hypocrite.

'I'd better be going,' she said.

'Yes,' he said, gesturing to the door. 'But a word before you go. It seems your friend has escaped.'

'H-has he?' Elsie quavered.

Sowerby stared at her silently for a moment, as if he had a rabbit in his sights, and was wondering in which direction it would run.

'The boy must be miles away by now,' he said at last. 'Which means there's nothing keeping you here any longer. You'll leave first thing tomorrow. One of my men will take you in a jeep.'

Elsie nodded speechlessly.

'I strongly suggest you don't come back,' Sowerby said in a calm, level voice that somehow far more frightening than any show of anger. 'This part of the forest is a dangerous place. Remember that.'

Forty-six

There was nothing to do but wait.

They had gone over the plan a dozen times. An hour before dinner, Mandeep would go to the building in the clearing and open the main door. Then, when Sowerby and his guests were sitting down to eat, John and Elsie would creep upstairs. While Elsie kept watch on the diners from above, John would unlock the cages using the device in Sowerby's room, although first he would have to open the window to allow the radio waves to travel. He thought that as the crow flew, the building was probably closer than it seemed. He might even be able to see its antenna over the trees. In the meantime, Mandeep would stay hidden for the night and make his way to the main road in the morning. One of

Sowerby's men would be taking the others back in a jeep, and John thought that, depending on who it was, there was a good chance he might be persuaded to stop and pick Mandeep up.

By the time Sowerby realised that the tigers had escaped, and his plans were wrecked, John, Elsie and Mandeep would be well on their way home.

They had discussed everything with Mandeep on the walkie-talkie, and told each other to be careful, and Elsie had said, 'I hope it works, it will work, won't it?' at least fifteen times, and now there was nothing left to do but wait.

They lay in their room, the walls golden in the evening sun. Elsie rubbed her nose. It had been itching the day before, and John had accused her of picking it. Now the itch was back, worse than ever.

'I wonder where the geckos are,' she said, to distract herself. 'Perhaps they only come out at night.'

John didn't reply.

'What's England like?' he said abruptly. Elsie glanced at him. He was staring up at the ceiling, his gaze unmoving.

'It's okay,' she said.

'It's not… like here, though, is it?' John said.

'No,' Elsie said. 'Not much.'

There was a long silence.

'You don't get to choose, do you?' John said in a bleak voice, his eyes still pinned to the ceiling. 'You just get born somewhere…'

'Or someone,' Elsie whispered to herself.

'And then—' John broke off.

They fell silent again, each busy with their own thoughts.

'It won't be so bad,' Elsie said at last. 'At least you won't have to go to school for nine months at a time. Terms are a *lot* shorter in England.'

'There is that,' he agreed.

'Plus, you've got all the stuff that's going to be invented to look forward to.'

'Fathead.'

'Thinhead,' Elsie said before she could stop herself. She covered her mouth to hide a giggle.

'*Thinhead*?' John sat up straight, outraged. 'There's no such word!'

Then they remembered they were meant to be thinking about the plan, and John flopped back down.

'I hope it works,' Elsie said. 'It will work, won't it?'

They ate supper in the kitchen, too tense to speak. Mr Agarwal hurried from saucepan to roasting dish, stirring and tasting with a look of harried intensity. On the other side of the table, the young boy who had served them tea that morning was laboriously trimming runner beans one by one, casting anxious glances at the cook.

The guests were due to sit down to dinner at eight. It was past seven now, which meant that Mandeep ought to have gone to open the door of the building, so the tigers could escape when they unlocked the cages. Elsie crossed her fingers under the table.

John had given up chewing his food. He was swallowing it whole, like a pelican. Elsie pushed a lump of her rice on to his plate and watched it disappear.

Finally, the meal was over. They pushed back their chairs and hastened back to the bedroom.

'We need to make sure Mandeep opened the door,' Elsie said. She rummaged under the mattress on John's bed, where they had hidden the walkie-talkie.

'I'll do it.'

'It's my turn.' Elsie twisted the dial on the front and heard it click. 'Hello, Mandeep?'

'You're meant to hold down the side button, remember?' John hissed.

'Oh, yes.' Elsie tried again. She heard a burst of static and then Mandeep's voice saying something.

'Have you done it?' she asked.

'Yes, although…' His voice grew faint for a second. '…but I opened it.'

Elsie took her finger off the button. 'He says he's done it,' she told John.

'I know he did, I'm standing right here, aren't I?'

John seized the walkie-talkie and thrust it into the waistband of his shorts.

Then, so suddenly that it made them jump, they heard a loud, ringing note that seemed to spread, like water after the throwing of a stone, and fill the air. It came again.

'What's that?' Elsie asked, although she had already guessed.

It was the gong in the hallway, summoning the guests to dinner.

Forty-seven

*E*sie lay on her stomach and peered through the banisters. She could see the whole of the dining room below. It was decorated in a grand, rather forbidding way, with wooden panelling on every side. Above the panelling were wrought iron light sconces, and the heads of several dozen deer, whose horns – some straight, some curved, some twisted – cast crisscrossing shadows over the white walls.

The dining table was in the centre of the room. The guests sat two on either side, with Sowerby at the head. Elsie was glad he had his back to her. She looked across to the turbaned bearer standing by the door at the far side of the room. Almost directly beneath her, a little to the right, was the entrance to the kitchen. As she watched, the cook's assistant came out with two bowls of soup and placed them hesitantly on the table.

'They're all there,' Elsie whispered.

John tiptoed along the wall to Sowerby's room, hesitated for a second, then slipped inside.

Elsie turned back to the diners. But nobody lifted their head. Even if they had done, she thought she was probably safe. It would be hard for them to see anything much beyond the circle of light. She inched forward, pressing her face against the banisters.

The sounds of glass and chinking cutlery drifted up from below, spoons rattling against china.

'What *is* it?' Marjorie said, gazing stiffly at her soup.

'Fish of some sort,' Nottle said. 'At least, I think so.'

Charles took a sip, coughed, and dabbed at his face with his napkin.

They had all changed for dinner, Elsie noticed. The men in dark jackets and white shirts, Marjorie in a blue, clingy dress with frills around the shoulders. Nottle's hair shone with an oily gleam as he bent his head.

'Or turtle,' he said. 'Could it be turtle?'

Sowerby said something to the cook's assistant, hovering uncertainly nearby with a jug of water.

'I'm told the soup is leek and potato,' Sowerby said.

'Jolly good! Ha! Ha! Ha!'

Even from this distance, Elsie could see that Charles's bow tie was far too large. It gave him the look of a bravely wrapped, but rather disappointing present. Something you would leave to the end, after all the other presents had been opened, Elsie thought, because you knew it was only a box of pencils, or a bottle of not very bubbly bubble bath.

'I'd really rather have some bread and butter,' Marjorie said. 'If that's not *too* much trouble.'

Elsie gave the door to Sowerby's room a worried glance. John had only been gone a few minutes, although it seemed longer. Perhaps he was having trouble opening the window. Or perhaps he didn't know as much about radio-wave devices as he'd made out and couldn't get the thing to work. Or perhaps she'd been mistaken, and it really *was* just a radio...

The soup was already being taken away, most of it untouched. Elsie wondered what Mr Agarwal would think. His assistant was clearly wondering the same thing. An air of doom hung over him as he removed each bowl.

She startled. John was back. He crawled towards the banister and dropped to his stomach.

'Did you do it?' Elsie whispered.

He nodded, his face alight.

'Are you sure?'

'I opened the window and flipped all the switches, waited a bit and then closed the window again.'

'Did you tell Mandeep?'

'Yes.' John was still clutching the walkie-talkie. 'Keep your voice down, they'll hear you…'

He was right, they had to stay quiet, although there was a lot more Elsie wanted to know. Like how long it would take for the tigers to leave their cages, and whether they would be far enough away by morning.

'I hope Mandeep doesn't bump into any of them,' she whispered.

'Not likely. They won't hang around. Even

drugged tigers can move pretty quickly.'

'I still don't understand—'

'*Shhh,*' John said.

Elsie closed her mouth obediently. She had been about to say that if the tigers scattered that quickly, she was even more baffled as to how Sowerby intended locating them next day. Even if he was only planning to give them a short head start, they would be hard to find. And he couldn't simply stay in the general area of their building as each one came out. Even the stupidest of guests would wonder why there were so many tigers in that particular corner of the forest. No, to be convincing, he would have to make a show of driving for miles in various different directions.

She remembered the way he had stared at the door, as if he could see her through the keyhole. And later, when he'd surprised her in his room, how stealthy he had been coming up the stairs. As though he had already known she was there.

Sowerby must find tigers the same way, Elsie thought. With his famous sixth sense.

Forty-eight

What Mandeep had been trying to tell Elsie over the walkie-talkie, before it cut out, was that as he was standing by the tiger's building, about to lift the bar and open the door, he'd had the distinct feeling that he was being watched.

It was almost night. Dark had already swallowed the forest, although there was still a lightness to the sky. Mandeep could see the outline of the clearing and the shape of the building, one shade blacker than the trees.

He stopped still, listening.

He was not alone.

Mandeep wasn't sure why he felt so certain of this, and it would have been easy to brush it aside as nothing more than his imagination. Yet he'd learned from experience never to ignore his instinct, because it was usually based on real things; tiny signals that he'd registered without even knowing he was doing so.

A certain quality of silence in the forest around him. Darkness where no shadow should rightly be. A shiver in the long grass that might have been no more than the movement of the breeze, except that the air was perfectly still.

Mandeep froze, his hand on the bar of the door.

The last of the light had gone, and the stars were hard and bright. Low in the sky, bigger than all the rest, the fierce spark of Mars burned gold as a tiger's eye.

Mandeep shoved abruptly at the bar, his heart pounding. He swung the door wide, made sure it was firmly wedged on the uneven ground, then took off across the clearing. The entrance to the path was impossible to make out. He hesitated for a terrified moment, then plunged into the bamboo, finding his way more by luck than judgment, not feeling the whip and tug of branches as he hurtled along.

It wasn't until he had stumbled over the twisted tree trunk and reached the relative safety of the main track that he allowed himself to stop. He bent, catching his breath, then straightened up and began walking fast towards the turning to the shrine and his hiding place.

The moon had risen, and the air was colder than it had been before. Mandeep hugged himself as he walked. Now that his panic had mostly subsided, he was beginning to regret his decision to hide in the cave. It had been comfortable enough during the day, and when John had warned him on the walkie-talkie about the guests, he'd been able to climb up the rocks behind the shrine and stay out of sight.

How funny Mr Gordon had looked, prodding fruitlessly into the cave with his cane!

Mandeep wished he could have signalled to Kelsie that he wasn't inside, although she would have probably given the game away. She had the sort of face that showed everything. He smiled to himself, remembering how she had wrung her hands.

He didn't know what to make of Kelsie. He wasn't even sure that was her name. John had seemed doubtful about it when he'd introduced her.

She was one of the nicest people Mandeep had ever met. And one of the strangest, although he couldn't put his finger on why he felt that way. Perhaps it was the fact that she was so easy to talk to. Or maybe it was all the peculiar questions she asked.

As if she understood everything – and nothing – at exactly the same time.

Mandeep reached the turning. He looked for the steps, even more treacherous in the moonlight, and thought how cold the cave would be. The outhouse wasn't pleasant, but there was a blanket there at least, and Mr Agarwal would bring him supper.

Mandeep suddenly felt very hungry. He had barely eaten all day.

The walkie-talkie in his pocket crackled, making him jump. He took it out and continued down the track, heading for the lights of the lodge.

Forty-nine

There was a lengthy gap between the clearing of the soup, and the arrival of the main course. Enough time for Gordon to get through two more glasses of wine, and for Charles to start playing with his napkin.

'Look, Marj,' he said, placing the knotted lump in front of her. 'A swan!'

On the other side of the table, Nottle had taken advantage of a lull in conversation to return to his favourite topic: HappyHappy Land and all its various delights.

John and Elsie listened from their perch above.

'Of course, business boomed during the war,' Nottle was saying. 'Nothing better than a theme park to take your mind off things. Worse it got, the more customers we had.'

'Sounds like you're sorry it's over,' Gordon said, giving him a hostile look.

'Oh, please,' Marjorie interrupted. 'Do we have to talk about the war *again*?'

John tapped Elsie's arm. 'We should go back,' he whispered. 'Wouldn't do to get caught up here.'

Elsie was about to agree when she saw the cook's assistant emerge, wheeling a trolley laden with platters, each covered by a large, silver dome.

'In a minute,' Elsie whispered. 'Let's wait until they start eating again and making more noise. They might hear us if we leave now.'

The assistant parked the trolley and began serving the table, his hands shaking, either from the weight of the platters, his own frayed nerves, or a combination of both.

'What on earth?' John muttered, as the silver domes were removed.

From a distance, it was hard to identify the forlorn items that lay beneath, only that they were virtually colourless and seemed to consist of nothing but tiny bones. And judging from the diners' expressions, it was no easier to tell up close.

'Some kind of small fowl, I believe,' Gordon announced finally, poking gingerly with his knife. 'Boiled, by the look of it.'

'I must apologise for the cook,' Sowerby said. 'He is new.'

'Not a bit of it,' Gordon said. 'I'm sure it's delicious, old chap. I must say,' he added, in a smarmy rush to change the subject, 'we're all looking very much forward to the hunt tomorrow. Isn't that right, Mr Nottle?'

'It certainly is. Can't wait.'

'I guarantee it'll take your mind off that theme park of yours,' Gordon said, smirking slightly.

'Unlikely,' Nottle said. 'Tiger Terror-tory is going to be *huge*. Our biggest draw yet. Nothing like pulling them in, eh, Sowerby?'

'Indeed,' Sowerby said.

There was nothing unusual about Sowerby's voice. He merely sounded bored. But Elsie's body suddenly stilled. She had the overwhelming sense that something significant had been said, by Sowerby, or perhaps by Nottle, only she couldn't work out exactly what it was. She frowned, trying to concentrate. What had they been talking about? It hadn't been anything important, simply idle conversation...

Marjorie's knife rang against her plate as she flung it down.

'I can't eat it. I simply *can't*!'

'Perhaps we can find you something else.' Sowerby gestured to the cook's assistant. He scurried away. There was a moment of silence, then a thump from the kitchen, as if something had been flung against the ground. Another thump, followed by a volley of words, each louder than the one before.

'The cook's blown his gasket!' John whispered, grinning. 'He's gone round the twist!'

Elsie wasn't listening. She had just realised what it was she had heard, and why it had seemed significant. And then, so rapidly that she couldn't believe she hadn't seen it before, everything that she'd been puzzling about fell into place. She rose to her knees in excitement.

'I know how he does it!'

'Who does what?' John was still grinning, his eyes fixed on the diners.

'*Sowerby.* I know how he finds them.'

She should have worked it out ages ago. There had been clues all along. Gordon in the jeep, talking about Sowerby's mysterious powers of communication. Sowerby with his tiger-skull clock: '*I've studied them for years using the very latest technology.*' The conversation she had heard through the keyhole, about a 'sixth sense' and sounds too low for the human ear to hear.

Elsie had wondered how Sowerby managed to find every one of the released tigers, without giving the game away, or spending days combing the forest. And now she knew. It had been Nottle's talk about 'pulling them in' that had done it.

Sowerby didn't go looking for tigers. He made them come to him.

'He uses infrasound,' Elsie said, tugging John's sleeve in her agitation. 'We can't hear it, but tigers can. He *calls* them, don't you see? It's like those whistles that only dogs can sense, only those are high pitched…'

John looked at her in alarm. 'Why are you talking so loud? Do you want them to hear you?'

'But you have to listen!'

Sowerby's voice drifted up from below.

'It seems the cook has abandoned us. Left the kitchen in a temper.'

'Disgraceful!' Gordon exclaimed. 'I hope you sack him on the spot.'

'Since he's left already, I hardly see the point.'

'But what about pudding?' Charles said in a plaintive voice. 'I was rather looking forward to pudding…'

Elsie tugged John's sleeve, even harder than before. 'You have to *listen*,' she repeated. 'I don't know what he uses to do it but—'

She broke off, struck by a terrible thought.

'The walkie-talkie!' she gasped.

It had to be that. On the day of the hunt, Sowerby would have one walkie-talkie. His bearer, back at the lodge, would have the other. It was how the bearer knew when to unlock each of the cages. But the walkie-talkies weren't the same, as Elsie had noticed when she first found them. One of them, the one she had kept – the one that Sowerby must surely use – was different.

It had a large red dial on the front.

Without speaking, without even thinking, Elsie lunged for the walkie-talkie that John was holding.

His fingers tightened reflexively. 'What are you *doing*?'

For a second, both of them had it in their grasp, each trying to wrest it from the other. Then it shot from their hands, straight through the banisters.

What was strange about the next few seconds was how slowly they seemed to pass. Elsie had time to notice how the walkie-talkie spun as it fell, and the precise point where it landed on the dining-room table, sending a glass flying in one direction, and the salt cellar in another. She tried to turn, but she was part of the slowness too; before she could move an inch, it was already too late.

The eyes of every single person in the room below were fixed in her direction.

'What the devil?' someone shouted. It was Gordon. He opened his mouth as if to shout again, but whatever he was about to say was lost, the words drowned by an eruption of noise from the kitchen. A series of ear-splitting screams filled the air, the clang and thunder of metal pans, a frenzied pattering of feet as if a multitude were on the move. Sowerby rose from the table with a look of fury.

'Monkeys!' John cried. 'The cook must've left the door open!'

A grey horde – too fast and too many to count – burst shrieking into the dining room, chairs tumbling in their wake. One monkey seized a handful of Marjorie's hair as it bounded off her shoulder, three more hurtled down the table, sending plates and glasses crashing. Others took to the air, leaping from deer head to deer head, their shadows crazing the walls.

The guests flailed their arms, trying to protect themselves. Nottle had fallen to his knees and was trying to squeeze under the table. Marjorie simply stood and screamed. Only Sowerby retained his presence of mind.

'Open the door, man!' he shouted.

The bearer on the far side of the room hadn't needed to be prompted. He was already swinging it wide. At once, the horde poured through into the hallway beyond.

The bearer slammed the door, his face grim.

'Something scared them,' John said. 'What on earth could have frightened them like that?'

Silence had fallen below, as if everyone was asking themselves the same question. Even Marjorie had stopped whimpering. She lifted a dazed hand to pat her hair, as though checking it was still there.

'Oh no,' Elsie muttered. '*Oh no!*'

Something had appeared in the doorway leading to the kitchen. A broad face, with ears pressed flat and whiskers at a wary slant. It paused. Then, with a roll of its massive shoulders, it stepped into the dining room.

Out in the open, the tigress would have looked big. Indoors, among the scattered dishes and flimsy chairs, she had the size and presence of a tank.

Fifty

The drink that Gordon was holding slipped from his hands with a tinkle of breaking glass. Someone gasped, and Marjorie, still clutching her hair, began to moan softly.

'Oh-oh-oh-oh.'

Yet the tigress seemed oblivious of the guests. She came on steadily, in an almost trance-like fashion, looking neither right nor left.

'Nobody move.' Sowerby's voice was hard as ice. His eyes met those of the bearer.

The bearer, showing extraordinary courage in the face of the animal bearing down on him, reached for the door a second time, ducking behind as he swung it open.

The tigress paced through and was gone.

John stared speechlessly at Elsie.

'That's what I was trying to tell you,' she said. 'It's the walkie-talkie. I turned the dial by mistake. It's calling them here.'

'Oh crikey!'

The words were scarcely out of his mouth when they heard a high-pitched shriek. A second tiger, closely followed by a third, had entered the dining room. As Elsie watched, it leaped on to the table, the wood creaking ominously under its weight, its paws sliding on the tablecloth, sending the remaining plates and cutlery tumbling to the floor.

A muffled crash came from the kitchen, and the sound of growling.

Panic seized the guests. With one tiger cutting off their exit to the hallway, and escape via the kitchen impossible, they pressed themselves against the walls of the dining room, all dignity abandoned. Gordon grabbed a chair and tried to brandish it in a threatening manner and hide behind it at the same time. Nottle bellowed for a gun. Marjorie cowered on the floor, biting her own hand.

Only Sowerby hadn't moved.

'Stay calm,' he ordered. 'If you stay calm, they won't hurt you.'

'They're bally tigers, aren't they?' Gordon shouted, still dodging behind his chair.

Marjorie removed her hand from her mouth. 'We have to stay *calm*!' she screamed.

A tiger crept under the table on its belly, peeled back its lips and hissed. In the kitchen, the growling had become a deep, panting groan.

John grabbed Elsie's arm. 'Come on!'

They ran to the landing at the top of the staircase and stopped. There was no sign of the monkeys. Going by the distant racket, they must have fled down the corridor and into the rooms beyond. Yet Elsie barely registered the fact.

The first tigress had left the hallway and was coming up the stairs straight towards them, moving so smoothly and so silently that she seemed to glide.

'Steady, steady,' John said, taking Elsie's hand. 'Whatever you do, don't run.'

They took a step backwards, and then another.

'No sudden movements,' John said. 'Nice and easy…'

Elsie didn't know how he could stay calm. She was gripping his hand so hard that she could feel every bone in his fingers.

The tigress reached the top of the stairs and paused, making a panting sound, her mouth half-open, saliva glistening on her black gums. Then she advanced.

Elsie felt her legs start to tremble.

'Steady,' John repeated, although there was a catch in his voice.

They kept going, still walking backwards, their eyes fixed on the tigress. As they passed the door to Sowerby's room, John pushed it wide with his free hand.

'Worth a try…' he muttered.

The tigress reached the open door of Sowerby's room and stopped, sniffing the air. Then she turned her head and slipped inside.

'Run!' John cried.

Elsie hadn't needed to be told. She was already making a dash for the staircase. As she flew by, she glanced down at the dining room. Someone had managed to open a window. She caught a glimpse of the guests jostling each other as they scrambled to escape.

'Through the main door,' John gasped when they reached the foot of the stairs. As they rushed across the lobby, he paused to grab his gun from the corner where he'd left it. Out on the verandah, Elsie heard running feet. Mandeep was there, his face bewildered.

'What is going on?' he said. 'What are the tigers doing here?'

'It's all my fault.' Elsie wrung her hands. 'I didn't mean to do it! I didn't know—'

She was interrupted by the sound of voices. The guests, having managed to extricate themselves from the dining room, were making their way around the side of the building to the relative shelter of the verandah, arguing loudly all the way.

Fifty-one

*E*ven in the dim light from the lodge, they made a sorry sight. Marjorie's hair stuck out at the side in a large knot, Gordon's glasses were crooked, and several buttons had popped off Nottle's shirt, exposing a wide swathe of his vest. They huddled at the bottom of the verandah steps, their eyes darting between the lodge, the looming forest, then back to the lodge again, as if unable to make up their minds what to do.

Marjorie was insisting they ought to retreat to the jeeps and lock themselves inside. But it seemed the bearer had the keys, and the bearer was nowhere to be seen. As they were debating, an engine started on the far side of the clearing, headlights pierced the darkness, and then were gone.

The bearer, like Mr Agarwal, had clearly decided enough was enough.

'The scoundrel!' Gordon spluttered, shaking an ineffectual fist. He caught sight of Mandeep staring from the verandah. 'That boy! It's him! He's behind all this, I'd bet my life on it.'

'We gotta get to our guns!' Nottle said.

'Yes, the guns, the guns,' Marjorie babbled. 'Go and get them, Charles.'

'But the place is crawling with tigers. I'm not fast on my feet, y'know.'

'Oh, you and your dicky leg!'

'It's that boy,' Gordon interrupted. 'He's to blame, I'd have had that *gaur* and the leopard too, if it wasn't for him…'

Sowerby's voice cut through the hubbub.

'All we have to do is keep quiet and stay together.' He was standing apart from the group, and Elsie noticed that he was holding the walkie-talkie. He must have turned off the signal, she thought.

'The tigers will disperse soon enough,' he said. 'In the meantime, I suggest we make our way to the servants' quarters.'

'That's on the other side of the lodge,' Marjorie protested.

'I assure you, we're in no great danger,' Sowerby said.

'Relief to hear you say that,' Gordon said. 'You're the tiger expert, after all.'

Sowerby lit a cigarette, his face expressionless in the flare of the match.

'But where did they come from?' Marjorie demanded. 'What are so many of them *doing* here?'

'They looked a little droopy to me,' Nottle said. 'Kinda disappointing, if you must know. Perhaps they were lost or something.'

'Never had tigers interrupt my dinner before,' Charles commented. 'Most unusual.'

'Maybe they were attracted by the smell of that food.' Marjorie wrinkled her nose in disgust. 'It was certainly strong enough…'

John had been following the conversation with growing incredulity.

'Don't you get it?' he burst out, finally losing control. 'How dense do you have to be?'

The guests stared at him, shocked. Sowerby's jaw tightened.

'I don't recall anyone asking your opinion,' Marjorie said.

'Sheer impertinence,' Gordon muttered.

'Hang on a minute,' Nottle said. 'Don't we get *what*?'

'The whole thing's rotten, completely rigged!' John cried. 'He trapped those tigers; he's been keeping them drugged so they'll be easy to hunt. Four tigers, one for each of you, don't you see?'

'That's a very serious accusation to make against a respected—'

'I'm telling the truth! There's a building in the forest, with cages. Take a look, if you don't believe me. The tigers came from there.' John paused. 'They must have… escaped somehow.'

A brief silence fell as John's words sank in.

'Is this true, Mr Sowerby?' Marjorie asked at last.

Whatever Sowerby was feeling, his face betrayed no trace of it. He took a drag of his cigarette as though giving himself a chance to think. Then he shrugged.

'You wanted to kill tigers,' he said. 'I got you tigers. And if things had gone smoothly, you'd have gone home with your trophies none the wiser.'

'We didn't know you were going to do it this way!'

'You had no idea how I was going to do it,' Sowerby said, flicking his ash. 'As I recall, you were all quite happy to hand over your money without any questions asked.'

The guests gaped at him.

'How dare you?'

'It's an outrage!'

'Hardly sporting!'

'You'll be hearing from my lawyers,' Nottle announced, puffing out his stomach to even greater proportions. 'Trust me. They're gonna make your life *hell*.'

'Living legend, my eye!' Gordon's whole body was stiff with fury. 'Once word of this gets out, there won't be a club in the country that will have you. You'll be finished, you'll be—'

He broke off. A tiger had appeared at the edge of the circle of light.

It was not like the others; a glance was enough to see that. Here was no drugged and bewildered animal. And there was nothing dazed about the way it was crouching, ears flat and haunches coiled to spring. It was by far the largest tiger any of them had ever seen, larger even than the one who'd lent its skull for Sowerby's clock, and its head had a scorched and blackened look, as if burned by its own fire.

The tiger bared his wet teeth, his eyes fastened on Sowerby.

Fifty-two

*A*ll day, the tiger had lain under cover, close to the foul-smelling building, his sleep disturbed and fitful. Humans had come, first two, then one alone, a small creature, filled with fear. The tiger had watched it stand and then suddenly dart away, noisy with panic.

All day he had listened – even as he dozed – to the growling coughs and calls of tigers just beyond. He lay pressed low to the ground, his tail twitching, feeling the tremor of their endless pacing like a pulse in his throat.

Then, after night had fallen, a new sound came. A distant, crooning hum, low enough to travel across rivers and over mountains and through the deepest of forests. The tiger raised his head, his ears pricked.

The call of his mother, commanding him to follow.

Throughout the apprenticeship he had spent at her side, from tumbling cub to full-grown animal, he had obeyed that call of hers. She had nursed him and protected him and killed for him, and taught him how to hunt, sharing her vast experience as he grew. He had learned how to survive from her. He had learned it by *following*.

The tiger hesitated for a moment, the tug of memory too strong to be ignored. He rose and crossed the clearing, heading in the direction of the sound, moving cautiously, acutely aware of the presence of others. There were tigers nearby, four of them. Two crossed his path without any sign of acknowledgement, their step sluggish.

The tiger had come across madness before, the stunned, erratic behaviour displayed by animals who had lost all sense of self-preservation. This was not that, but it felt too similar for comfort, and he drew back instinctively, keeping

his distance as they carried on ahead.

He was approaching the second clearing, where the large building stood, when the call abruptly stopped. The tiger paused and gathered himself. He was dangerously close to humans – a great many of them. The air was tangled with their scents, oil and charcoal and metal and sour sweat. There was nothing to be gained by going any nearer, and everything to be lost.

He was about to turn away when he caught another scent, mingled with the rest. It was only the second time he had come across it, but he recognised it instantly. For as long as he lived, it was a scent he would never forget.

Burning tobacco, sickly-stale.

The smell of death itself.

The tiger felt rage tighten every sinew. He had been noiseless before, but now a different kind of silence seized him, deeper and a thousand times more lethal. He crouched and began to advance, his body slippery in the darkness, as if his touch had turned the air to oil, his gaze on the circle of light beyond.

Humans in a group, huddled like deer, the one he sought standing apart. He could feel the liquid of their fear. It flowed towards him in rivers, joining the ocean of his rage until it crested into fury.

The tiger opened the cavern of his mouth and roared.

Fifty-three

There were no words to describe the sound of that roar, if sound was what it was. Elsie felt it as much as she heard it, the way an avalanche vibrates the bones or thunder twists the gut.

The tiger's contorted face was even more terrible. It was nothing but a gaping mouth, its forehead vanished, its eyes squeezed to slits, still locked on Sowerby, standing in his path.

Sowerby's whole body had tensed. Even the bones in his face had tightened. As if the tectonic plates below the surface of his skin had shifted in some impossible way, creating ever steeper cliffs and chasms of his features.

Without turning his head, without even seeming to move his lips, he spoke.

'You've got the only gun.'

Elsie glanced at John, beside her on the verandah.

'Shoot it,' Sowerby said.

John reached for the rifle at his shoulder.

'*No*,' Elsie said in an anguished voice.

'Slowly, slowly.' Sowerby's voice was deathly calm. 'Aim for the heart, boy.'

'No,' Elsie whispered. '*Please…*'

She had stopped John from shooting the tiger. She had *stopped* him. But that didn't matter, it was going to happen anyway.

'You mustn't, you *can't…*'

Nobody heard her. She might as well not be there.

'Do it,' Sowerby said, panic entering his voice for the first time. 'What are you waiting for?'

John's finger groped for the trigger, the rifle stock trembling against his shoulder. Elsie shook her head desperately. He wasn't looking at her. Nobody was looking at her. Not even the tiger. She was just an extra, forever in the background, someone not meant to change the past, or make any kind of difference.

She felt a sudden sense of injustice, so strong she almost cried out.

It isn't true!

Without thinking, ignoring the gasps around her, she marched down the verandah steps, passed the cowering guests, and kept going. Six paces from the tiger, she stopped. John couldn't shoot it now, she was standing in the way.

She lifted her chin and looked into the tiger's burning eyes.

And the tiger looked back. It looked at her as only a tiger can, with an unblinking, total gaze. As if it saw the whole of her complete. As if nothing in the world existed except for her.

Elsie knew she was frightened, almost more frightened than it was possible to be. But her fear was a separate thing. It was standing next to her, and along with it, all the other things that made her who she was. All her hopes and loves and secret sorrows. Everything that had ever made her laugh, or cry, or wish one day could last for ever and another could end before it began. Her failures and her victories, and all the moments – the very many moments – that lay in between, when she had looked for the silver lining and made the best of things.

It was all there, so close Elsie could have reached out and touched it. Yet she didn't.

I haven't been born, I don't exist, I am Kelsie Corvette, whose voice can tame the savage beast.

Elsie drew a deep breath. Then she opened her mouth and began to sing.

'*There's a dark and a troubled side of life,*
There's a bright and a sunny side too…'

Her voice, as Mr Nunes had so painfully noticed, was squeaky and out of tune. Yet it was utterly steady.

'*Tho' we meet with the darkness and strife,*
The sunny side we also may view.'

Around Elsie, nothing moved or breathed. Even the leaves on the trees were still, as if astonished into silence.

'*Keep on the sunny side, always on the sunny side!*' Elsie's voice rose as she came to the chorus. She had only been allowed to hum it before, so she sang extra loud to make up.

'*It will help us every day, it will brighten all our way,*
If we keep on the sunny side of life!'

Fifty-four

*T*he tiger halted, partly out of surprise, and partly because the sounds coming from the tiny human were so disconcerting. They reminded him in a vague, half-forgotten way of the mewling cries of a hungry cub. But what mainly stopped him in his tracks was the creature's total absence of fear.

Aside from encounters with other tigers, he had never in his life come across an animal that hadn't displayed some degree of fear – from bristling caution to outright horror – in his presence. Fear was a living thing, the spark that fired him to action and fuelled the blaze of his anger.

Now its absence had the opposite effect, like a lull in the wind that settles the long grass. The tiger's tail stilled, and his lip uncurled.

Of all the legends ever told about his kind, there was only one that was true.

In the distant past, being small, and weak, and full of fear, man made a gift to the tiger. The gift had been created out of dreams, shaped by longing, polished to a shine by terror. It was the gift of extraordinary power.

The tiger became a god, gods rode upon its back, the souls of dead heroes lived within it. It could fly through the air, magically appear and disappear, kill with the force of its gaze alone. Its eye was full of luck, and its heart full of courage, and its bones could cure a thousand ills.

Being small, and weak, and full of fear, man gave the tiger extraordinary power.

And then, being small, and weak, and full of fear, he wanted it back again.

So, man tried. He plundered the tiger's body, and ground its bones, and took its skin to wear, and stood for photographs above its corpse, as if to say: *I have it! See? It is mine!* But nothing worked. The corpse was just a corpse, and the pages turned on all the photographs.

The tiger's gaze shifted from Elsie. He looked into the forest, thinking of the miles still to be covered before he reached home. He knew, without knowing, that his power was not something that could be given or taken away. It could not be found among his bones, or in a trophy's sightless eyes because it was not there. Only in the beating of his heart and in his living, secret self.

He swung his head, the light gleaming for a moment on his copper hide.

Then he was gone.

Fifty-five

*F*or a good thirty seconds after the tiger vanished, nobody moved or made a sound. They stood as though they had forgotten they had mouths for speaking, or legs for walking, or even brains to process thought.

Then Marjorie gave a juddering sigh, as if she was pulling her breath up in a bucket from the depths of a bottomless well.

'I'm going to faint, I'm going to faint!' she cried. 'Oh, Charles, on our *honeymoon...*'

Immediately, as though breaking from a trance, everyone started talking at once.

'Is it gone?'

'Did you see the size of that thing?'

'The girl, singing to it!'

'Damn foolhardy, if you ask me.'

'Reckless, ought to have shot it while he had the chance.'

'Kelsie!' Mandeep's voice rose above the noise. 'Kelsie! Are you all right?'

Elsie heard his feet on the verandah stairs. John was staring at her with a look of such stupefaction that she thought she might break into hysterical laughter, the kind that went on and on and didn't stop until someone slapped you. But she couldn't. The itching had started in her nose again, only it wasn't itching any longer. It was more like burning.

Elsie clapped her hand to her face. Her whole head felt as if it was on fire. A wave of pressure rose in her chest.

John and Mandeep were beside her.

'What's wrong?' John said. 'Are you hurt?'

Elsie shook her head. The pressure had reached her throat now, it was climbing higher and higher. She shook off John's hand and stumbled blindly away, out of the light, across the clearing. Her foot caught the root of a tree and she staggered, eyes watering as though squeezed by some inner, unstoppable force. She drew a gasping breath –

And sneezed.

PART 3:

What Happened
Instead

Fifty-six

1948. KRUGER PARK, SOUTH AFRICA.

If Sowerby had tripped over his lace almost anywhere else, he would have suffered a scraped knee at worst. He would have got to his feet with a curse, tightened his boots, and been on his way. But he was crossing a precipitous ridge in a lonely, mountainous area when it happened, and he immediately flew straight over the edge.

As he hurtled down the steep slope, loose rocks tumbling around him, he had time to reflect that he had had nothing but bad luck since that disastrous episode at the lodge, two years before. His savings gone in legal fees, his lectures cancelled, his possessions – what was left of them after the tigers and monkeys had finished rampaging through the building – seized by the Indian authorities, his reputation ruined, even as far afield as here in South Africa. He had time to think too, of the remoteness of the region and the unlikelihood that his body would ever be found, even if there was anyone in the world who cared to look for it, which there was not.

He even had time – because it was a very long slope – to marvel slightly at the irony that he, who had brought down scores of the world's most terrifying predators, should be brought down in his turn by nothing more ferocious than a dangling boot lace.

Then a boulder, bouncing off the side of the hill, hit him on the head and all his thoughts were done.

His body was discovered less than half an hour later by three lions. They had been alerted by vultures who clustered at a safe distance as the lions fed. What the lions and vultures left, wild dogs found. A family of hyenas took the bones and armies of ants and assorted beetles hauled away the tiny scraps that remained. By the time the last, microscopic crumb had gone, it was impossible to count how many creatures Sowerby had nourished, or how many lives in which – however briefly – he had played a vital role.

He had finally become what he had prized above all else.

An object of value.

Fifty-seven

1977. NEW DELHI, INDIA.

*M*andeep shifted in his seat on the stage as the speaker at the podium made his introduction. The conference hall was packed with people, although he had no trouble making out his mother, sitting in the middle of the front row, looking both pleased and vaguely disapproving as usual.

Mandeep's hand crept up to straighten his tie.

The speaker was taking a long time to get to his point. Mandeep sighed to himself, his mind wandering. Back through the years, to all the events that had led to this moment. The papers published, the speeches made, meetings with influential people, lucky breaks and unexpected setbacks, obstacles overcome.

Before that, years of unrelenting study, scholarships to universities, qualifications earned... Mandeep smiled, thinking of the letters that had gathered after his name. Yet he knew that none of it would have been possible without the support of his family and his teachers, plus his own stubborn, unshakeable determination.

And a string of pearls, given to him half a lifetime ago.

Mandeep could remember every detail of that afternoon. It was the day before the Lassiters were due to leave India, and Mrs Lassiter's room was still strewn with clothing and partly packed trunks.

'Come,' she had said, as Mandeep stood awkwardly in the doorway. 'I have something for you.'

And before he could protest, she had unhooked the string of pearls from around her neck and was pressing it into his unwilling hands.

He shook his head, surprised and embarrassed. 'I can't, it's not—'

'I want you to have it. You pulled John from the river. You saved his life, Mandeep.'

He shook his head again.

'Please,' Mrs Lassiter said in a voice he had never heard before.

He looked up. There were tears in her eyes.

'I couldn't have lost another child,' she said. 'I think it would have... killed me.'

She paused, trying to smile, then took Mandeep's hand and curled it tight around the string of pearls.

'One day, when you have children of your own, you'll understand.'

The pearls were fastened with a diamond clasp and extremely valuable. After they had been sold, there was enough money for a train ticket to the city and for Mandeep to enrol in a good school, although he had to work two jobs to stay there, waiting on tables and hauling boxes of groceries before returning home to study until late into the night.

The speaker was finally winding to a close. Mandeep heard the sound of his name and the thunder of applause. He stood up, his mind still far away.

The string of pearls had helped to set him on his path, but something else had been even more important. A scrap of paper he had found near the ashes of a long-ago campfire.

Kelsie had left it there. The girl with all the peculiar questions. She had stared down the biggest tiger in the world with nothing more than a song, and then simply vanished. They had looked for days without finding her. She must have run away from home, John said, although nobody knew where that home might be, or how she could possibly survive alone in the forest.

Mandeep had never forgotten that girl, nor the words written on her scrap of paper.

What is an ecosystem? ran the typewritten question.

And beneath, in scrawling pencil, the misspelled answer.

An ecosystem is a commewnity of living organisms that interakt together because they are all linked in a kind of cercle circle of life and everything needs everything else or else it will all just eventchually die.

Mandeep still had that piece of paper, tucked away in a drawer in his office. He'd heard the term 'ecosystem', of course, though not until decades later, and he would never understand how Kelsie had known about it all those years before. But her words had seemed like a message.

The applause was dying away. Mandeep cleared his throat.

'As you know,' he began, 'the government has recently announced the designation of another area of national parkland.'

A picture flashed up on the huge screen behind Mandeep's back. A winding track through groves of sal trees, the sun pouring in great columns of light between the ancient branches.

His forest.

'It is my pleasure,' Mandeep said, and for all his practice at public speaking, his voice caught for a second. 'My *great* pleasure, to present to you India's newest tiger reserve.'

The area was small, not nearly large enough. But it would be added to, it would grow. Others would take up the fight. Mandeep closed his eyes for an instant. There would be many in the years to come, he was sure of it. People who believed as he did, who shared the same dream. The dream he had held in his heart for as long as he could remember.

Of the forest as a garden, with a place for everything, and where every living thing was safe.

Fifty-eight

1989. ENGLAND.

The train driver opened the door of his compartment and settled into his seat with a slight creak of his back. The seat was old, its leather worn from decades of use, so moulded to the shape of the driver's backside that it felt like a part of his body itself.

Which in a sense it was. He had sat in that seat almost every day for the last thirty-nine years, barring holidays and sick leave.

Yet not for much longer. As the driver started up the engine and the train pulled out of the station, he was pleased that his last day on the job had turned out to be a sunny one. It gave everything he saw a bright clarity, every sleeper in the tracks stood out, every passing cottage, every tree. But perhaps it only looked that way precisely *because* it was his last day.

Days were like pennies, the driver thought sadly. They only rattled when there were hardly any left at the bottom of the jar.

Thirty-nine years. He knew every bolt in the tracks, every curve, every copse of trees. They were flying by him, vanishing, already gone...

He was coming to the long bend, with the village below him on the right and the hill rising steeply to trees on his left. For thirty-nine years he had driven his train along this precise stretch of track, and for almost all of them, the same memory had flashed without fail through his mind.

How could it not? It was stamped there, as firmly as the shape of his backside in his seat.

July, 1956.

He'd seen a splash of colour on the tracks ahead. A toddler, his face upturned, as if pinned in place by the sight of the train hurtling towards him. The driver had been dimly aware of shouting from the carriage behind him, the sound of fists beating against a window. His hand shot to the brake, then froze.

He couldn't apply the brake, not at the speed he was going, not on this bend. The train might run clear off the tracks if he did. And even if he were to risk it, there was no chance he could stop in time. The child was so close, the driver could already see the stripes on his tiny jacket, his curly hair lifting in the breeze…

A movement caught the corner of the driver's eye. He glanced swiftly to his left and his mouth fell open.

A man was running down the slope to the track in a long diagonal. He was moving fast, faster than seemed possible, fast enough to keep pace with the train, fast enough to actually *overtake* it.

For a second, the driver's brain was unable to take in what he was seeing. Then he felt a surge of terrified disbelief. The sound of beating fists in the carriage behind grew suddenly louder.

He can't do it! The words were a shout in the driver's head.

The fool! The brave, crazy fool!

In the hours and days and years to come, the driver would be asked over and over again to describe what happened next, although he could never give a satisfactory answer. At the very last instant, when impact seemed inevitable, he had tightened his eyes in horror. He had not seen the speeding figure cross the tracks with barely seconds to spare, scoop up the child, and tumble to safety on the other side. But the driver had imagined it many times, and each time he did, he thought the same thing.

If that man hadn't been there, in just the right time and place, the child would have been killed. And the driver would have blamed himself for it for the rest of his life.

He shook his head. The child had been saved, no harm done.

He rounded the bend and the village and hill disappeared behind him. How fast that man had been, the driver marvelled for the ten thousandth time. How he had *run*!

As if running was what he was meant for.

Fifty-nine

THE PRESENT. ENGLAND.

*E*verything was the same, except there was less of it.

Elsie was too dazed to move for a second or two. Then she slowly lifted her head. The green house door was still ajar.

Uncle John was standing on the threshold, looking at her.

'There you are, Kelsie,' he said.

'I sneezed,' Elsie said numbly.

How old he looked, and yet not old at all. She could see the boy in him quite clearly, still twelve years old, despite the wrinkles. Time had changed him, and time had left him just the same.

'I told you my nose was itchy,' Elsie said. 'You said I was picking it!'

Uncle John laughed. 'Did I?'

He doesn't remember, Elsie thought. It was seventy-four years ago, after all.

'I think there must have been a bit of pollen in there,' Elsie said. 'And it came out when I sneezed.'

Uncle John walked up to her, moving steadily without a trace of a limp. They stood for a moment, looking down at the flower that catches time. Its leaves had turned brown and its curling petal had withered to the colour of a cobweb.

'You're right, Kelsie,' Uncle John said at last. 'It must have been the pollen.'

'You don't have to keep calling me that,' she said. 'I made it up, you know.'

'But it's your name. I gave it to you myself.'

Elsie stared at him, bewildered.

'When you were born,' Uncle John explained. 'I was going to name you Elsie, after my mother, but then I looked into your eyes and I thought, *it's her*! So, I added a K.'

'I was going to suggest "Corvette" as a middle

name,' he continued, 'only I didn't think your mother would go for it.'

'You *recognised* me?'

Uncle John nodded. 'I'd been wondering for some time when you'd show up.'

'But you didn't believe me when I told you I came from the future!'

'I know,' Uncle John said. 'And I went on not believing it. Then it occurred to me that if someone your age really *had* come from the future, they'd probably have just as much difficulty explaining things as you did. Then the moon landing happened.'

Uncle John smiled. 'And the first female prime minister, and the explosion of plastic... by the time the internet made its appearance, I was thoroughly convinced.'

Elsie couldn't speak. Her brain was too busy trying – and failing – to work the whole thing out.

Uncle John put his hand on her shoulder. 'We can talk about it later, when you've rested,' he said. 'Colleen has made pancakes for breakfast!'

'Colleen?' *The girl in the photograph*, Elsie thought. The one Uncle John had been in love with.

'But I thought you never saw her again.'

'I never saw her again?' Uncle John repeated. 'You mean to say—'

He broke off, shaking his head. 'I told myself I wouldn't ask questions. To know what would have happened in your life if things had turned out differently, might be rather... terrible, don't you think?'

Elsie nodded.

'So, you married her after all,' she said. 'How did it happen?'

'I'll admit, to begin with I didn't have much of a chance. There were a lot of other people in love with Colleen, you know. But then there was that incident with her nephew.'

'What incident?'

Uncle John made a face, scratching the back of his head. 'I managed to save the little chap from an oncoming train. Sheer luck, but it seemed to change Colleen's whole outlook. Thought I was some sort of hero. Lot of nonsense, of course.'

'So, you did it,' Elsie said wonderingly.

'Did what?'

'Your one amazing thing.'

'Lot of nonsense,' Uncle John repeated, although she could tell he was pleased by the way he rushed to change the subject.

'You didn't do so badly yourself,' he said. 'With that tiger, I mean. I thought you were a goner for sure.'

They left the greenhouse and walked down the path by the side of the house and through the back door into the kitchen. Colleen was at the stove, twice as wide as the girl in the photograph, but just as merry of face.

'Mandeep!' Elsie cried. There was a picture of him on the wall where the ceremonial Gurkha swords had been. He was dressed in a suit, shaking hands with a group of important-looking people.

'We've kept in touch over the years,' Uncle John told her. 'Colleen and I went to visit him in India not that long ago. He's a grandfather now.'

He pulled out a chair at the kitchen table, and Elsie sat down with a grateful thud. Until that moment, she'd not been aware of how terribly tired she was, nor how terribly hungry.

She was Elsie with a K, who had faced down an elephant and sung to a tiger and avoided at least ten giant spiders and seen the statue of a god in a silent glade. And she still didn't know how any of it had happened.

After breakfast and a good, long rest, she would have to find a fresh notebook and write the whole thing down. *The Incredible (True) Adventures of Kelsie Corvette.* She already knew how it would start.

Chapter one

Most people would have screamed to find a tiger in Uncle John's spare room but Kelsie meerly raised an eyebrow. How very peckuliar, she thought to herself...

Colleen placed a plate in front of her. It was piled so high she could barely see over the top.

'There's plenty more if you want seconds,' Colleen said.

Uncle John gazed thoughtfully at the stack.

'You can't go wrong with pancakes,' he said.

A Tiger for All Time

THE PRESENT. CENTRAL INDIA.

The cub was less than a year old, yet he was nearly the size of an adult, the sole survivor of a litter born in the root pit of a fallen tree. One sibling had died soon after birth, another had been taken by wild dogs six months later. Only the cub was left to follow his mother, looking where she looked, stopping when she stopped, each step a silent echo of her heavy, velvet footfall.

He might have been her shadow, but for the unusual markings on his head, stripes so broad and black they made his face look scorched.

They had fed the previous night. A full-grown boar. His mother had held it down for her cub to make the kill, his grasp clumsy, his teeth grappling against the boar's bristly neck in an ecstasy of eagerness. Hours later, the memory was still fresh in his mind as he moved through the grass, the morning sun on his shoulders, keeping his gaze on the two white patches behind his mother's ears as she walked ahead.

He felt a vibration in the ground, a distant, rumbling growl, becoming louder by the second. His mother paused and raised her head. But it was neither threat nor prey, and certainly no reason to alter course.

The cub had heard the sound many times in this part of the forest. It came from humans in vehicles, moving back and forth along wide trails that skirted the meadows and the densest trees. They appeared singly, or in groups, either inching along or else travelling so swiftly that the dust spat and turned to cloud. Yet fast or slow, alone or together, they always did the same thing when the cub and his mother happened upon them.

They stopped. They fell quiet.

It was no different that morning. Two vehicles,

motionless on the trail, as the cub's mother emerged from between the trees. She crossed in front of them without sparing a glance, the cub at her heels.

The vehicles were no more than a leap away. The cub caught the bitter scent of humans, heard the sound of their breathing, full of strange gasps and mutterings. His mother had already disappeared into the thicket, but the cub was young and easily distracted. He had never come this close to humans before. He halted mid-stride to look at them.

Instantly, all movement in the vehicles ceased, all breath. As if the turning of his head had stopped the world itself.

For as far back as anyone in the area could remember, there had been a tiger that looked like this cub, one in every generation. A male, massive in size, with the same burned-black striping on his face, the same air of command. So identical were these animals that even the wardens of the park, who monitored each birth and death, half-joked that they must be a single individual. And that was perhaps why, unlike all the other tigers in the park, the wardens never gave this one a name.

He was simply *the* tiger. Part-real, part-legend, born over and over with the rising of the sun. A tiger that would live for ever, as long as there was prey to stalk and forest deep enough to hold him.

And people who would fight to keep his world from vanishing.

The cub stared at the humans in a silence so profound that he could hear the sigh of the dust settling on the trail. Then he glanced aside and continued on his way, walking the tiger's solitary path. No wider than the length of his whiskers, no louder than the snapping of a twig. Where his feet fell the softest, and the cover was greatest, and the light tricked every eye but his.

Acknowledgements

As always, special thanks to my agent Rebecca Carter whose steadfast support makes all things possible, and to Fiona Kennedy, eagle-eyed Jenny Glencross, and the whole team at Zephyr.

Huge thanks also to my sister Thomasina Unsworth for her endless love and encouragement, and for being the funniest, most enthusiastic and long-suffering partner in adventure that anyone might hope for.

I could not have had two better guides to the Indian forest than naturalists Karan Singh Kotla and Sanjay Mohan, both of Pugdundee Safaris. Their passion, depth of knowledge and unfailing good humour will never be forgotten.

Last but not least, in gratitude to all the dedicated men and women who work – often at great personal risk – to protect wild tigers and ensure their future.

Tania Unsworth,
Boston,
March 2020.

JOIN THE FIGHT

'Wild cats, their prey, and the natural habitats on which they depend are in peril and we need your help. If you think you are too young to be heard and make a difference, remember that some of today's most prominent and impactful conservationists, like Greta Thunberg and Mya-Rose Craig, are but teenagers.'

John Goodrich, Chief Scientist and Tiger Programme Director, Panthera

Of all the big cats, the tiger is the closest to extinction. Worldwide, less than 4,000 remain in the wild, and their survival is precarious. Hunted for their body parts, facing loss of habitat and dwindling supplies of prey, tigers need protection more than ever.

You can be part of the fight to save them.

Learn more by visiting the websites listed below.

Follow and share. Raise money – either by yourself or as part of a team – and make a donation to your favourite tiger conservation group. Tell everyone why tigers matter.

Mandeep is a fictional character, but his dream is real. I hope you'll make it your dream too.

Tania Unsworth

Panthera: Panthera's Tigers Forever Programme is working to increase tiger numbers by at least 50% across Asia.

Find out how you can help at panthera.org

World Wildlife Fund: For great fundraising ideas, including how to symbolically adopt a tiger, go to worldwildlife.org

Wildlife Conservation Society: Learn how WCS works with local governments to protect tigers at wcs.org

Centre For Wildlife Studies: Dig deeper into the science behind tiger conservation at cwsindia.org

Now enjoy reading

The Girl who thought her Mother was a Mermaid

Out now in paperback

One

The first time Stella Martin ran away, it was in her sleep. The second was by accident. But the third time she did it on purpose, to find out whether she was human or not.

The sleepwalking began when she was eight, soon after her mum died, and at first Stella didn't get any further than her bedroom door. The moment she touched the handle — which had always been slightly loose — it rattled and woke her. One night, though, the door was left ajar and there was nothing to stop her passing through, into the silent, carpeted corridor beyond.

She padded down the broad staircase, across the hall, into the kitchen where the marble countertops, polished by Mrs Chapman every day, gleamed liquid in the moonlight. Out of the back door she went, on to the patio, moving without hesitation, as if on command.

The grass was wet from the sprinklers, but Stella didn't seem to notice the chill on her bare toes. She stepped on to the lawn, still fast asleep, passing through the circle of light from the porch lantern, moving into deeper and deeper shadow. When she reached the low stone wall, she swung her legs over, her feet finding the flagstones on the other side.

Ten metres away lay the swimming pool, its water black as flint.

It was lucky Stella's dad was having another of his sleepless nights. Luckier still that, sunk in his trance of sorrow, he had forgotten to lower the window, and happened to catch sight of Stella's fluttering white nightgown. Even so, he was almost too late. Stella's body was tilting towards the water when he caught her around the waist and pulled her to safety.

Stella's mum had loved the pool. She had been a superb swimmer. It wasn't just that she was fast, there was more to it than that. It was the way she used to move. As if she was made of water itself.

She had taught Stella how to swim. Stella could remember the feel of her mum's hand cupping the back of her head. Her mum's smiling face blocked out the sun, and her hair glittered at the edges like a red-gold crown.

I've got you, she had said, as Stella hesitated. *I've got you.*

Stella raised her body and suddenly she was floating. Her fear had gone. For a moment, staring wide-eyed at the sky, she felt as if it would never come back. Her mum had taken it away; the fear Stella had, and all she would ever have, even if she lived to be a hundred years old.

But after the sleepwalking incident, Stella didn't want to go swimming. The sight of the pool frightened her, and she was glad when her dad finally had it emptied and covered with a heavy tarp.

'Such a waste,' Mrs Chapman said, casting a disapproving look at the dead leaves on the surface of the tarp. 'And all because of a little sleepwalking! Do you recall what you were dreaming about?'

Stella nodded. She had been dreaming she was in the pool. It was daytime. Reflections danced against the white walls and bottom of the pool, holding the water in a shimmering net of light. The net would hold her too, she thought, as she waded further in. But a cloud passed over the sun and the net vanished, and there was suddenly nothing beneath her reaching feet. The bottom of the pool had disappeared and she was sinking, deeper and deeper. She twisted her head and looked up. The surface of the water was already far away, the light dwindling. Below her desperately kicking feet she sensed nothing but a vast emptiness. She was descending fast, unable to stop or cry for help, down, down, to a place so deep and dark that she could never come back...

Stella opened her mouth to explain all this to Mrs Chapman, and then closed it again.

'Well?' Mrs Chapman prompted. 'What was it?'

Stella didn't know how to describe the feeling of the dream, the panic. 'It's a secret,' she said finally.

Mrs Chapman ruffled Stella's messy hair. 'What a strange girl you are!'

Stella didn't argue. Mrs Chapman ran the house. She cooked their meals, and kept the floors spotless, and knew where everything was. And if Mrs Chapman said she was strange, it was probably true. Stella was filled with a mysterious dread.

It was exactly the same as the terrible, sinking feeling in her dream.

Zephyr is an imprint of Head of Zeus.
At Zephyr we are proud to publish books you can read and re-read time and time again because they tell a brilliant story and because they entertain you.

Subscribe to our newsletter to hear all the latest news about upcoming releases, competitions and to have the chance to win signed books. Just drop us a line at hello@headofzeus.com.

@_ZephyrBooks

HeadofZeus

www.readzephyr.com

ZEPHYR